SHOT *through the* HEART

Shot Through the Heart

CONTENTS

CONTENTS

BLURB

♥SHOT THROUGH THE HEART♥

Two opposites. One chance rescue that leaves no chance of stopping our chemistry.

Coming from a family of all boys who play hockey, all I ever wanted was to be *seen* by my dad. When he offers me an opportunity to intern at his startup sports magazine, I jump at the chance to impress him. It's not until after I'm given my first assignment that I find out the catch.

I must write a *hit piece* on his rival team.

It shouldn't be too bad. It's not like I'm friends with these guys.

Enter Noah Miller.

AKA: The Team Flirt.

Actually, I should first introduce his jaw line, and then you'll understand my flustration. No, that's not a typo. I'm 100% flustered when he's nearby.

Never fear because my super-shield instincts tell me to resist him at all costs. It won't be too long, and I'll have this hit piece done and dusted.

Problem: He's handsome.

Again, I point to the jawline.

More infuriatingly, he has the super talent of rescuing me. It would be swoony if I wasn't tasked with destroying his team.

No one—especially Noah—is worth ruining my chance of finally making my dad proud of me.

Not even when Noah saves me one more time.

Or another time after that.

Why is he so good at that?

It's absolutely maddening!

Shot Through the Heart is a closed-door-yet-swoony-eyes romance that delivers an all-things-hockey-and-wholesome romcom.

One

Paisley Anton

For the record, I'm not a mosh-pit girl.

My glasses easily slide up when I adjust them—again—as the bridge of my nose is slick with perspiration. My pores are leaking like a sieve. I'm dead center in the middle of a mosh-pit brawl, and I'm sucking air as I leap the highest my petite little legs will shoot me.

I was told this was a charity sports gala—but this is clearly not what I had envisioned. I had thought of a relaxing Friday evening with classical music. Not this event. This is a high-cardio concert with a live rock band. All I can say is I'm glad I opted for my trusty combat boots with my dress.

While we are getting things on record, I will say I'm not a dress girl either. The dress is the same garment I wore to my great aunt's funeral last month. It's black—the hue of rebellion I always wear—and void of any embarrassing ruffles or form-fitting stitches.

I had left my hair down in long waves until I got so sweaty that I forced it into a messy bun by haphazardly shoving a pencil through the top of a twist in a Jurassic-period-style bone hairclip.

It's clear I'm not here to *enjoy* this mosh pit.

I don't mosh pit, and I definitely don't dance.

I'm the invisible girl behind the camera, who is on an undercover assignment.

Now I'm jumping for my life.

Elbows fly at me from every direction, and I tuck my camera protectively in my armpit like a football. It's the magazine's new Canon, and I don't have enough for even a down payment to replace it. I cut my gaze to the left, pining for an exit.

These people are giants, creating a canopy of arms and hands boxing me in. It feels like one hundred and eighty degrees here, and all the brutes are hogging the oxygen. I cut my gaze the other way, hoping I can duck out of this pit. My chest constricts as panic seeps into me.

I'm surrounded.

"Excuse me!" I yell at the couple in front of me with the assertive tone of the strong woman I am. It's a guy I don't recognize standing behind a girl. They are jumping in unison, and I'm not surprised they don't hear me. I don't know how anyone can hear when we are about three feet from the massive speakers.

My breath grows shallow as the air gets weaker down here.

I need to get out!

I inhale deeply and step forward until I'm butting up against a woman. Before I can explain that I'm only trying to maneuver around her, some massive person moshes into my back, knocking me down, my glasses flying off my face and out of reach.

You'd think the immediate circle of people around me would scatter, but they don't notice as they continue to mosh, trapping me down. I weave my hand around sets of ankles, grappling for my glasses, but people keep shuffling, and I'm blocked. Sweat pours off my forehead. I crawl forward, barely missing my glasses as someone nonchalantly kicks them out of reach *again*.

This was a terrible idea.

I pant, inhaling a deep breath, and stretch my arm in aim for my blacked-framed glasses once again, but this time a big shoe finds my palm and stomps down on it like it's a landing pad. I cry out in pain, waiting for the crunch of my fingers, but by some miracle, none of them break. My sobs fall on deaf ears, drowned out by the ear-splitting music. Desperation sets in and I try to stand, but I get shoved back down by the waves of people pushing forward. I open my mouth to scream for help when a set of strong arms wrap around my waist and tug me up. At first I freeze, bracing for impact again. I'm thinking it's another blow.

"Guys, get out of the way!" a mysterious deep voice hollers. "There's a girl on the floor."

It's as if the mysterious-voice guy knows the magic words, commanding instant respect, and the crowd parts. He drapes my arm over his shoulder and props me up, yelling in my ear, "Lean on me, and I'll get you out of here."

My breathless body flops forward, fully allowing my rescuer to drag me out of there. The crowd behind us quickly closes the gap as if I was never there.

The invisible girl behind the camera.

The one who captures all the moments but is never *in* them.

How fitting that they don't even notice when I leave.

We burst through the ballroom's double doors, with me still hanging onto this guy's neck like one of those ragdoll doorknob hangers. My hero looks at me with warm auburn eyes.

Eyes I'd know anywhere.

I've shot them many times.

Horror music hums in the background of my mind.

Dun dun dun.

It's Noah Miller, winger for Granite Ice.

The one everyone calls the pretty one.

He obviously knows it too because he's a huge flirt.

I glance up at him, taking in his thick dark hair and a steel-cut jaw I could cut a perfect bagel on. For a hockey player, he leans on the trim side but has the usual broad shoulders. He is the most handsome player on the team—*too bad I'm dead-set on destroying his career.*

I'm visiting Mapleton as an intern for my dad and his sports magazine *Sports Era*. It's more of a mission to put together a spread for Granite Ice, a barely known but up-and-coming AHL team. That sounds normal, but where it gets interesting is Granite Ice is owned by my dad's arch-nemesis—Bill Baker.

This is the chance I've been waiting for my whole life—a chance to impress my dad, who has always treated me as his invisible child. I am the only girl out of four kids in my family, and my brothers followed in his footsteps to play hockey. I love hockey, but I'm not built to play it. I took up photography to get involved, taking shots of all my brothers playing, but even though I was always right outside the rink, I yearned to see that proud gleam in my dad's eye that he offered my brothers.

He says he's proud, but it has never been with the same tone he gives my brothers.

"Where do you want me to take you?" My hero's gruff voice pulls me from my assessment.

Embarrassment shoots to my face and heat radiates through my cheeks. I have nowhere to look but away. Thankfully, he's not one for chatter, and his gaze sweeps back to the ballroom as if he's in a hurry to get back inside.

"Oh, ah . . ." I nearly choke on my saliva as I scan the empty hall, squinting without my glasses. "Here's fine." I point to the wall, allowing my body to slide against it all the way to the carpet floor. I'm still a little too woozy to stand, and my head feels as if it's spinning.

"Are you sure you're okay?" He hikes a curious brow and patiently waits. The tips of his hair appear damp with sweat from the heat of the dance floor. I zone out, staring at them, wondering what it would be like to run my fingers through them.

Cough.

What was I thinking? Boy, I really did almost lose my sanity in that mosh pit. I would never do that!

He's a classless jerk, like all the rest of the guys on his team as evidenced by how they all nearly killed me by stomping me to death. Who has a mosh pit anymore anyway?

My dad's right.

I lock my jaw forward, lowering my eyebrows into my mad face. Someone needs to put a stop to these arrogant jerks. I force out a strong voice. "I'll call a friend."

"Take it easy." He slides his foot away, and I watch him strut back through the door. Even though he's fully clothed in trousers and a blazer, his arm muscles annoyingly protrude out, showing off his sculpted biceps, and the ripples keep rippling all the way up to his neck.

Nobody needs that many muscles.

I shake my head as disgust builds in my chest. He shouldn't be allowed to casually walk around with all those muscles. He's going to hurt someone with those. I bet they aren't even real. He probably has one of those inflatable muscle suits underneath his jacket just to be a showoff. That's all these Granite Ice guys are. Just fake balloon muscles with no brains. I seethe, as my hand still pulsates from getting stomped on. I can't even flex my fingers.

As soon as he's gone, I drop a giant sigh of relief.

So glad he's finally out of my sight.

Cradling my hand, I scan the hallway. My head jolts all the way back. *I don't have my camera!* My hand flies to my face. *Or my glasses!*

My gaze cuts to the door, but I'm not going in there. I'll never come out alive. I suspected this sports gala was going to be interesting, but I didn't think it would ignite this fire in my gut to get even. My blood nearly boils as I think about how all these guys had no problem stomping on me as if I was a lifeless rug.

There's only one thing I can think of.

These brutes must be stopped before they kill someone.

Two

Noah Miller

Funny how I had hoped we would actually win a game. We were mired in a losing streak, but I thought we had turned it around.

I was wrong.

It's been a grueling third period, where we can't score to save our lives. We've had plenty of shots, but they are blocking everything we send to the net. With my knees bent, and my stick positioned to catch the puck, I skate backwards toward the opponent's net, determined to get open. My heart expands, pounding hard against my ribcage, as I align myself with the net. My gaze bounces from their defense man to our team center, Axl, who has the puck.

Axl flicks his wrist, sending the puck soaring right to me, and I grab it on the backhand.

The crowd instantly jolts into cheers, but it doesn't steal my concentration.

My adrenaline spikes, fueling my speed to skate into the slot and shoot the puck toward the net. Their goalie is as wide as a truck and blocks the puck, and his defenseman quickly ties me up, keeping me from getting to the rebound. Axl skates over and takes control of the puck, and this time he cuts around the back of the net and then charges out front. Determination etches in the lines of his face.

The crowd screams, and their chants create a cacophony of sound that makes my heart pound even harder. Axl shoots the puck, and it flies toward the net. Their goalie kicks out a pad in a flawless block, and the buzzer blares, signaling the end of the game. Nobody from our team shares a victorious expression.

The home crowd goes silent. Their eyes are glued on us as we skate off the ice with neutral expressions, fighting to conceal our disappointment. Once again, the scoreboard blares the truth of our failure.

I skate toward the tunnel, irritation rising as I spot the press lined up and taking photos. I don't understand why they want pictures of the losing team, and I certainly don't want my big mug on any social media headlines. I'm not a narcissist in any way, but my stepdad is always on my case about keeping up our image. It's clearly more about him than me, because he's got a lot at stake as the team owner.

No matter what I do, it's never good enough, and having my losing face go viral is going to upset him. I turn my head as I skate off the ice and do my best to push past the barrage of cameras. One of the photographers has her phone up, and it's obviously aimed at me. I put my hand up in front of her as I walk past, but not before she clicks the photo button.

For a split second, our eyes meet. Her feral blue eyes spiral back at me, daring me to do something, and my cheeks heat up. "You can delete that," I growl, but she turns away, pretending to not hear me. Or maybe she is too interested in grabbing more shots of the guys as they skate in. I continue down the tunnel but shoot an angry look over my shoulder in time to catch her glancing back at me, and I repeat, "I'd appreciate it if you don't post that."

Her face morphs from indifference to impatience as she shows me her phone screen with the photo. "Can't," she huffs, clearly struggling to have patience. "I'm on assignment to get photos of everyone, and I'm running out of time. If you want me to delete this one, you'll have to stand there and pose nicely for me to get a better one."

My eyes narrow. She seems awfully familiar. Her dark hair is tied back in a low ponytail, and she's wearing a black sweater that does nothing to tell me how I know her. She is striking in a way most girls would dream to be—a natural beauty with no noticeable makeup—but she looks too young to be working for any news media. "Assignment from where?"

"Sports Era Magazine." She lowers her phone. Her gaze tips toward me in a slanted angle, and she continues, "I'm doing a spread on your team, and I had a bunch of photos already, but I lost my camera last night. Now I'm cutting it close to the deadline, so I need to keep your photo."

A shock of recognition jolts through me.

I know her.

Her fiery sapphire eyes had begged me not to make a big deal out of her condition. I was so disgusted that people were stomping on her. I wanted to scream at everyone, but those eyes begged me not to while also somehow pulling me to her.

"Hey, you're that chick from the gala." I flick my index finger out as my brow furrows together in concentration. "The one I pulled out of the mosh pit."

Pink flares fire under her freckles as her lips part, and I have the exact same sensation I did at the gala. I have a strong desire to protect her.

"Hey, how are you?" I reach out to touch her forearm but yank it back as I catch myself. With everyone watching, this could easily be misconstrued, especially if a photo is taken. I don't want to embarrass her, but I also feel terrible that I left her in the hall by herself. I had trouble sleeping last night because I kept wishing I'd stayed with her until her friends came. Those pleading eyes haunted me every time I even tried to close my own.

"I'm fine." She dramatically crosses her arms in front of her.

I scan behind her and see that the arena is clearing out, and nobody seems to be waiting for her. "Are you here alone?"

Her eyes round, but they are unwavering as she quips back, "Yeah. I'm working, remember?"

She's got sass. I'll give her that. Tilting my head, I'm about to rephrase my question, but Coach Carlson calls from behind me. "Hey, Noah. Are you coming?"

"Yea, I'll be right there." I glance around at him and then shift back to the girl.

"Bye." Her voice is monotone. Unengaged. Irritated?

What did I ever do to her . . . except rescue her.

"Make sure you delete that photo," I call over my shoulder as I make my way down the tunnel.

"I'll get right on that." I sense a tad bit of sarcasm in her voice but don't turn back as Coach has his gaze pinned on me. I pick up my pace to the locker room, ready to get an earful of "tough encouragement."

Not by the coach. Carlson is a great guy.

But by my stepdad—Bill Baker.

Three

Paisley

A semi-truck smokes past me, the gush of air rocking my little Toyota on the icy road, and I grip the wheel with both hands until my car steadies. It's right after the hockey game, and although I was able to shoot the game with my phone, I'm still desperate to find my camera.

Earlier in the day I had returned to the ballroom, only to find that the room had already been restored to normal. All evidence of the party was gone, including my camera and glasses. I don't even care about my glasses as those are replaceable, and I'm easily able to use my contact lenses until I get a new pair.

I inquired with the event coordinator about the camera, but she told me that no one had turned in a camera. She took my information in case it turns up, but she also said not to get my hopes up. At this point it's not even the monetary value of the camera that stresses me out, but I need those photos!

With a deadline looming in two weeks, most people might give up.

But not me.

I won't give up looking for my camera, but I'm going to figure out a way to make my deadline with or without it. With a lump in my throat, I head back to my Airbnb for the night. My foot is firmly on the accelerator, but my speed declines. I scan the dash, and my heart sinks. The fuel light glows on E. I had seen it flash on when I got in earlier, but I was in a hurry to get to the game early so I could get a good seat for photos. I knew I could go a while with the light on.

Clearly, not this far.

My brow dips. Just once can I catch a break?

I grit my teeth as my car slows even more, and I yank on the steering wheel, pulling onto the shoulder. While shaking my head and sighing loudly, I rummage through my purse on the passenger seat and locate my phone—which is dead.

Not even 2% for me to send a text.

I wore down all the charge taking photos of the hockey game. I don't even have a charger in the car. Giving up, I jab the hazard lights button in the center of my dash and throw my head back hard against the headrest.

Just great. It's my first job, and it feels like I'm destined to fail.

Working for Sports Era Magazine is my dream job. Sure, my dad pulled his puppet strings to land me this cushy job with one of his brands, but all I ever wanted was one chance to show my dad he can be proud of me too. He's one of those dads that believes in pulling yourself up by your own bootstraps, and that's his reasoning for not helping me out financially. He makes a point to remind me often that I would be working in food service if it wasn't for him. I get it. I want to be able to do this on my own, but it's a lot harder than I thought it would be. I blink back warm tears, a glaring reminder of how much I hate that I'm struggling so much.

It's not for lack of trying either.

I've been working my tail off to gain a lot of resume-building experience as I smile my way through an assortment of events and games. Recently, Granite Ice has been in the news because of a relationship between the team center and a celebrity. When I mentioned to my dad that I wanted to cover the story, he became unglued. He's not a yeller, but he started muttering so many random stories, I knew something was up.

Facts I learned about my dad this last year.

One: He hates Bill Baker.

Um, that's pretty much it.

So maybe not plural *facts* as much as it is just *fact*. He said the only way I could come out here to cover this story was if I exposed them. It's not an ideal assignment, but with the economy in a dumpster fire, I know people who are in much worse situations.

I zip up my jacket, pulling the fur-trimmed hood tight around my head, and I wrap my scarf twice around my neck, covering my mouth. If I must walk back to town in these frigid temperatures then I guess that's what I'll do.

I grab my door handle and push hard against the winter wind gusts, all the while biting back a sarcastic smile that says *it can't get worse than this.* I put one heel to the street and wince. I'm not the type of girl to wear heels, and my shoe selection alone screams how hard I'm trying to succeed.

A black SUV flies past me, and I quickly jump back. This two-lane highway suddenly feels really narrow. Instead of continuing, the SUV hits the brakes, coming to a stop on the shoulder a few car lengths ahead of my car. Relief floods my chest. Even though I had been resigned to walk, I'd much rather catch a ride. I shut my car door, taking a moment to lock it, and turn back to the SUV. My celebration doesn't last long as I jolt into a frozen stance while familiar humiliation washes over me, warming my cheeks.

Strong-set jaw.

Placid thick lips.

Dark hair that curls around the bottom of his Granite Ice beanie.

Noah Miller.

Again.

What are the odds?

I throw my hands up in exasperation. This isn't the kind of break I was looking for. It's just making the situation even worse. Seconds tick before I break my glare and shake my head, backing away from my car.

Why can't a nice old grandpa find me?

"Did you break down?" He gestures as a huge gust of wind blasts me, making me wobble on my heels. I'm never wearing heels again. I drop a sigh, as if it hurts to confess my error.

"Ran out of gas."

A wide knowing grin grows on his face. "I can give you a ride back to town if you want."

No, I sure don't want to do that, but apparently what I want doesn't ever matter.

I dart a glance over my shoulder, estimating how far I'd driven. I think it's about six miles to the nearest gas station. Not an issue at all if it was nice out, and if I wasn't in heels. The wind howls around me, piercing at my exposed fingers, and I curl them into fists and stuff them into my pockets. My right hand—the one that got stomped on—throbs out its own heartbeat. It's only a hand, but it adds to my overall feeling of overwhelm. I hate this situation with everything in me.

I look back at Noah, then down the highway.

Six miles in a car is less than five minutes, and then I can be on with my night. I cut my gaze back to him, and he seems to be studying me, as if he's already making up a rebuttal to any defense I would offer.

I might as well take the ride.

I flick my hair back, but it's useless because the wind whips it back around my face. I look at him, silently pleading for him not to make this awkward. "Ah, if it's not a bother, I'll take a ride to the gas station."

He nods, flicking his gaze back to his car, and without any more words we rush toward it, as it seems like the weather is getting worse by the minute. After slamming my door, I'm hit with the scent of new expensive leather. It sort of makes me hate him a little more as his life is so picture-perfect, while mine is drastically imploding. He cranks the heat and then shifts the car into gear, pulling out. It's cringe quiet, and I slowly allow the breath I'd been holding to leak out of my lungs.

He keeps his gaze on the road. "Where are you headed?"

Warmth returns to my face, flushing with heat. I'm unsure if it's a reaction to the cold, the humiliation over my situation, or maybe a third embarrassing option of my memories of being stomped on at the gala flooding back. I fiddle with the ends of my long hair, pulling it over my shoulder, and nervously comb the tangles with my fingers. "Back to my Airbnb."

His jaw twitches, drawing my attention back to it. It's a shame all the jerks get the best jawlines. I drop my gaze and focus on pulling the loose string on my scarf. One minute down.

"Did you know there's a winter storm advisory?" His tone is friendly, but yet so irritating.

I seal my lips together as I fight to keep all my secrets inside. Like how I hate him, and I'm only here to destroy his career. "You can take this exit." I point out my window, fixing my gaze on the truck stop, a beacon calling me back to my sanity.

He pulls into the truck stop entrance and parks in a spot right up front. He gives me a sideways stare. Before he has a chance to offer, I yank on my door handle, relief already rushing into my lungs with the icy air. "I'll be right back," I mutter. The place is fairly crowded with trucks waiting out the storm. It takes me a few minutes to grab a gas can and fill it. I'm back in the car in less than five minutes, and we drive in silence back to my car. Noah parks behind my car. "Can I help?"

"I got it from here." I'm already sliding out of my door, so thankful to get out of here. "Thanks for the ride."

"You bet. See you around—"

I slam my door, shutting off his sentence, and murmur, "Not if I can help it." I tug the strings on my hood, pulling it tight around my head as I walk back to my car. I'm so glad that's over. I hope I never run into him again like that.

Four

Paisley

When I originally reached out to Bill Baker about doing a spread on his team, he graciously offered to arrange a small office space in the Mapleton Arena, where Granite Ice plays. It's been perfect because I get all kinds of behind-the-scenes access to the team. Plus, it's past the janitor's closet, where nobody goes, so it's super quiet. Not surprisingly, this spot has quickly become the place where I do my best editing.

I spent all Monday morning taking photos of practice and got nothing incriminating, which was a super huge disappointment. After lunch, I return to my office, but as soon as I open the door, I halt.

A beautiful camera sits on my desk.

My camera.

Seeing it's all in one piece brings a giant sigh, and I plop into my chair and pick up the camera. There's nothing to indicate who dropped it off. I assume it was the lady from the hotel. I'm sad I missed her stopping by, because I owe her a huge thank you. I'm so grateful to have it again.

My shoulders fall, releasing all my tension. At least I know the photos didn't end up in the hands of someone else. Not to mention, three weeks of my hard work would have been lost. Add on the embarrassment of getting stomped on at the gala, and it would have all been for nothing.

I turn the camera over, examining it. The lens falls into my hand, and I see a long crack right up the center. My stomach sinks. I can replace the lens, but it's not cheap. My stomach drops even more as I continue my examination. Sure enough, the onboard flash is missing. Again, I can replace that as well, but this is getting expensive. I turn the camera over to open the memory card slot, but the compartment is wide open.

The cover is broken off and the memory card is gone!

Cold sweat frosts my back as dread floods over me. *I celebrated too soon.* I shake my head at how stupid I am for not backing up the photos. Who doesn't do that? It wasn't an accident, either. In my arrogance, I didn't want to put them on a computer because I didn't want the photos to accidentally get leaked. These photos can be highly incriminating to me.

I sigh heavily. I want so badly to impress my dad, and he trusted me with this assignment and this camera.

The one time he gives me a real shot, and I blow it.

There are two things—and only two things—I know: hockey and photography. If I can't get this assignment right, then I'll never get anything right. With my deadline looming, this spread needs to be completed and sent to my editor, Steve. If the assignment was to cover people, I could call them up, but I can't schedule extra hockey games because I lost the shots.

This is bad.

I clasp my hand over my chest, fighting the waves that want to send me into a full-blown panic attack. I set the camera back on my desk and place my hands firmly on the desktop when something rustles behind me, and I raise my gaze.

A man stands in the doorway, his hand propped up on the doorframe. He is wearing a beanie pulled down low, covering his ears. I immediately recognize his deep voice when he greets me, "Hey."

He's clearly lost.

Or I'm seeing things.

I squint, like I'm practicing for the optometrist. I'm wearing my contacts, but there is no way this is happening.

Eyes.

Yep, same eyes. Dark. Not scary dark like he's a shapeshifter or something. Just puppy dog dark but almond-shaped. I like almonds.

Yep, and they are on his face where they were the last time I saw him.

Lips.

He's got some of those, too.

They are smirking at me right now.

And a dimple right below his smile crease that points back to his smile. It's the perfect little button that makes it hard for me to be mad at him because it's just so cute.

That dimple isn't fair.

My gaze looks behind him for a random clue of why he's here, but he's alone. There's no reason anybody would be back by my office, as it's strictly out of everyone's way at the end of a dead-end hall. I speak to him as if he's no more important than the random fly who is buzzing around my desk. "Are you lost?"

His feet stay firmly on the ground, not moving. "I'm looking for you."

"Me?" I hike a brow, suspiciously eyeing him. The only other time I had someone down here looking for me was when they scratched my car in the parking lot, and they got my name after the police looked up my plates. "What did you do?"

"Ah, nothing. I don't think." His eyes dart side to side before returning his gaze on me. "I was checking on you. I'm Noah. I guess I should have led with that."

I slowly raise a brow, contemplating what to do with this experience. "Noah," I echo as if he'd spoken a foreign language. I heard him quite clearly actually. I have perfect hearing, but I'm still so confused. The earth could split open, and that would be less shocking than this moment.

It's one thing to accidentally stumble across me three times, but there is no way Noah Miller came to see me on purpose.

His stance seems intentional. He's here for something. As I pause, I almost slap the side of my face. "Ah, right. Hockey photo.

I can delete it if you're going to make a big deal about it." I reach for my phone, and I mumble, "I lost all the other photos. It won't matter if I'm down another one."

"What are you saying?" He takes an uninvited step inside my office, and he crosses his arms over his chest. His gaze cuts to my camera, and he tacks on, "You have the other photos from the game."

My facial expression flattens as my senses alert to his nearness. He's so close I swear I can smell a recent black coffee wafting off him.

Smells amazing.

That's not fair either.

I like coffee.

And I didn't have enough for this encounter today.

I slowly set my phone back down. "I have photos from the last game." I say the words like a confession. It's so hard to accept responsibility in this life-imploding moment of failure. "No photos from any of the previous two games, because I lost my camera at the gala."

"You didn't back them up?"

"I didn't," I squeak out, careful not to disclose too much. I offer him a lazy one-shoulder shrug, but I don't know how I manage to hide the fact that inside my chest I'm having an actual heart attack.

All my work is gone.

"That stinks."

"Yeah." My heart ticks up a notch as I try to protect the project as much as possible.

"Is that why you insisted on keeping bad photos?" He stuffs his hand in his Granite Ice jacket pocket and gives me a side-eye.

"Are we still hung up on that?" I grab my cell phone again and don't stop until I have his photo. "Look." My finger hovers over the garbage can icon as I hit delete. "Gone. Can you sleep now?" I roll my eyes to heaven at this pretty boy who can't handle a less-than-perfect photo of himself.

"I sleep just fine . . . but thank you."

"Alright." I pull my brows up, feeling the exhaustion of this conversation seeping in. "Have a nice day."

"Huh?" His feet stay cemented on my floor, and he makes no attempt to leave even when I cut a glaze to the open doorway.

"Well, I deleted your photo. You don't have to worry anymore." I grit my teeth, wondering how one person can be so concerned about his image. *I have bigger issues going on.*

He's silent as he rocks back on his heels. He's clearly cocky because of his superior athletic abilities. His presence has this vibe that I can't place, but it makes my nerves twist, akin to nails on a chalkboard.

"I wasn't here for the photo," he asserts. "I came here to see you."

"Well, you see me." I look away, embarrassment still clawing its way up my throat. Of all the people to find me failing at life, does it have to be Noah Miller? I resist the urge to slam my head on my desk and pray he moves on.

"Maybe I came at the right time because I can help." He gestures forward. "Maybe it's not all lost yet. I can message some of the guys. I'm sure their families have photos they can send to you."

"I can't ask for help." I grab my throat as my airway is tightening. "I'd have to admit I lost everything. Do you know how embarrassing that will be?"

"Look, ah . . ." His eyes pace my face before his lips bend down. "I don't even know your name."

There it is.

The biggest truth bomb of them all.

I'm invisible.

Not just to my dad, but to most people.

In high school, I skipped choir every day for a month to test this theory, hoping just once someone would notice my absence. Didn't work. Since nobody ever noticed my presence, I wasn't missed or even marked absent. I graduated with a record of perfect attendance.

I thought things would be different after high school graduation, but it's just more of the same. I spent weeks stalking this team, going to all their practices and games, but nobody even noticed me. Like slamming my head against a brick wall, the sound of this truth bomb echoes all around me. I lower my gaze to the floor, warm tears welling in my eyes, but I shut my eyelids tight.

Stillness fills the room, seeping in a heavy cloud of tension. Noah dips his head, peering at my downturned face. "I didn't hear you."

I bury all my emotions, determined to hold my wounds deep inside. I nod, asserting myself with a strong breath. "My name is Paisley."

"Nice to meet you, Paisley." He pulls one side of his lips into a crooked smile, revealing his perfect teeth. "I can ask my teammates. It shouldn't be hard."

What is this encounter all about anyway?

Why is he even bothering me?

I deleted his photo.

I narrow my eyes, looking for clues to what he's really after, but again, all I notice is that everything about him is handsome.

That's not fair, either.

Of course he comes here all handsome.

That's what flirts do.

I steel my jaw, resisting his charm, but a narration plays in my brain.

Really, very, incredibly handsome . . . like so, so very nice looking and—

"What do you think?" He interrupts my thoughts, but I'd forgotten his previous question.

"*Handsome,*" I blurt out as confusion bubbles in my gut and rises slowly up my chest and into my throat until I cough and then blubber out, "I think you have a handsome . . . *wall* behind you."

A snort bleeps out of his nose. Not like a growling animalistic one. It's like the ones I sometimes emit when I think I've eaten the last chocolate chip cookie, but find a half broken one hiding in the bottom of the box.

He raises his palm to his chin and rubs it, his expression forgiving of my blunder and void of any sarcasm. "Should we stop wasting time and get to work?"

I want to ask him why he is helping me.

But his offer to help couldn't have come at a better time, and he's right. We are wasting time. "Ah, sure." I grab a pen and note pad, positioning myself to scribble. "I'll make a list." This earns me a raised eyebrow of what seems to be respect. *A very demure-looking eyebrow of respect.*

Noah retrieves his phone from his jacket pocket and starts to scroll, and he starts listing names. "I got Jackson's number." He rolls in his bottom lip and quietly sends off a text. I write Jackson on the notepad.

He confirms once his text is sent, and he resumes scrolling. "I got Axl." His voice drops off as he sends his text, and I add the name to my list.

"And I have Emma, Lexi, Shayla, Ashlyn, Aspen, Raleigh, Blakely, Brooklyn, and Lena—all cheerleaders," he says, his voice monotone as if he doesn't realize the *massive* list of cheerleaders' names he just rattled off.

My jaw practically hits the floor. "Why do you have so many cheerleaders in your phone?" I can't help but blurt. His head jolts back, as if he's remembering who he's speaking to, and his eyes widen. "Answer the question." I playfully aim my pen at him like a sword.

"Ah, I have everyone's number because I'm on the team." His expression stays flat, and he tacks on, "And it's an old phone."

I blink, not buying this excuse at all, and drop a curt, single-word reply, *"Sure."* I add, *The entire cheerleading squad,* to my list and give him a side-eye. Under my breath, I add, "Boy, you really are the team flirt."

"It's not like that at all." His cheeks flame red, and he puts his phone down.

I place my pen on the pad, and I risk a personal question. "So, you have a lot of friends, huh?"

"I guess. I mean, I live in town. It makes sense I know people."

"Right." I inhale the quietest breath as it burns deeply to hear how his life experience is so vastly different than mine. I get it. There are popular people, but it's never been my experience. I'm quiet as we work through the rest of my list, adding names and numbers that Noah has from practically every hockey fan in town. After about thirty minutes, I place my pen next to the last name on my list. "We should have what we need for game photos. I need socials though. Do you have any gala photos?"

"Ah, sure."

"I only need a few group ones." It's time for my now ritualistic side-eye. "Don't give me the whole cheerleading squad."

"I got a bunch." His fingers dance over his phone keyboard, and he pulls up a series of photos. Even though he's a good three feet from me, I can see they are all group photos when he flashes the screen at me. "What phone number can I forward these to?"

I take his phone and insert my number, knowing I'll be just another person in his personal Rolodex of every single female in town. "I guess we got everything, then." I let out a sigh of relief as I admire my list, and then check the time on my phone. It's time to go, so I walk over to the computer and tap on the mousepad, moving my cursor to the bottom of the screen to shut it down as I'm taking my computer back to the Airbnb to work on my page spreads. Pivoting on my heel, I head to the coat hook on the back of the door. "I, ah, can't thank you enough, but I'm glad we are done because I'm starving."

"You're welcome." He stuffs his hands back in his pocket and a gleam sparkles out of the corner of his eye, forewarning me. "Now you have to make it up to me."

My heart slams against my chest as I blurt, "What?"

"You said you were hungry. Let's go grab something to eat."

A trickle of goosebumps run along my spine. I have zero desire to hang out with any of these Granite Ice guys. However, if I go with Noah and put up with his ridiculous flirting, I might be able to find out some more dirt on the team . . . and that's an opportunity I can't pass up, especially since I'm way behind. "I like food." My heart motors hard against my rib cage, and I enforce a face of steel trying not to add a devious smile.

I know what I'm up to, but his gaze lingers on me long enough for me to start to wonder *what he's really up to.*

Five

Noah

I was over the photo, but I had a lingering residue of Paisley's fiery eyes imprinted on my brain. It had me wandering down the hall of the arena, hoping for a glimpse of her. When I found her in need of help, I didn't hesitate because it gave me every excuse to be near her. Now, I steer out of the parking lot, rolling through the stop sign while I toss a glance over my left shoulder and check my blind spot. "Where do you like to eat?"

"I'm not picky." She offers a lazy shrug as her feet shuffle in front of her as if she can't get comfortable, and I roll my bottom lip in, hoping she's nervous because she feels this magnetism too.

"Red Barn Kabobs?" I offer a team-favorite place right on the edge of town. I risk another glance in her direction and suck back a hard breath as I catch her looking back at me with those fierce blue eyes firing all the light. There's no color equivalent on the planet, and it's hard to not study them.

"They have the best barbecue chicken. Tender and juicy inside. Crisp and not too flaky on the outside." Her automatic reply hints she's done some heavy analytics on her food reviews. Most likely she's a foodie.

"Or what about The Grove?" I throw out another place to make sure she isn't being agreeable to be nice. This place is also super inexpensive. I try to watch my budget, since I live off my AHL salary like the rest of the guys. And, I'll say it aloud for the people in the nosebleed sections, it's almost nothing.

"They have the best curly fries." She nods, pursing her lips. "Crunchy and the right amount of salt."

"Is that a yes or a no?" I slow my speed, since I'm coming up on the turn to Red Barn's, and I don't know if I should take it yet.

"Neither. It's just fact. You can pick what you want."

I sigh in relief that she doesn't seem too high maintenance. I can work with this. "Since you like the chicken from Red Barn and the fries from The Grove, we'll go to both places. Now the question is, who has the best desserts?" I hold my grin in while I wait to see her reaction as I already feel like I'm going to get a weighted response.

"JD's Cheesecakes." The inflection in her voice mirrors that of someone cracking a life-saving code. "They have *the* cheesecake." Her voice lowers into a secret-sharing volume. "You know the one. It's cheesecake with a brownie crust, and that should be enough to make a perfect dessert, but then when you bite in, it explodes your mind because it has coconut hidden in the center."

"Brownie explosion." A chuckle moves up my throat, as that's the cake that made JD's famous in the New England states. "I guess we are going to *three* places."

"If we are doing all three, we should start with Red Barn first," she instructs, the conviction in her tone confirming she's a serious foodie. "I have all the apps so I'll order ahead. That way we can just pick everything up." Her gaze is already locked on Red Barn's website. "What do you want?"

I study her face, not wanting to miss her animated expressions. "A number four."

"We have one thing in common." Her fingers dart over her phone screen, adding things to our virtual takeout bag. "Ordered." She confirms and drops her phone to her lap.

"Perfect plan."

She smiles a coy smile that lights up her whole face. "Planning is sort of my thing."

"I'm starting to see that about you."

"What about you?" Her expression turns a tad sour. "What's your thing?"

"My th*ing*..." I drag the word out, placing emphasis on the last half of the word. "I just play hockey and procrastinate everything else."

"So, procrastination?" She tucks a long strand of her dark hair behind her ear, and it contrasts with her pale skin so much that it's strikingly beautiful. She continues, "I'm a planner, and you're a procrastinator. Not sure we can be friends."

"It might be rough." With a slight smirk on my face, I put my blinker on, take a sharp left, and slow the vehicle to a stop in the pickup lane. I roll down my window. When the server hands me the drinks, I pass the first one to Paisley and wait for her to take the first sip.

"Yep, they still have the best soft drinks in town," she quips as she finds the cup holder in the center console.

"All right, let's get the fries next." I pull out of the drive-through and turn back onto the main road, steering toward The Grove.

A comical grin pulls on the edges of her lips. "I've never had three places to eat for one meal."

I make a right turn into The Grove as their parking lot is adjacent. I find their drive-through empty and go right to the window. We only wait another minute for the bag, the fumes of grease wafting in my car, and we both steal a glance at the bag. "We are eating those now, right?"

"I was hoping." She chuckles, unrolling the bag with extreme determination laced on her face and grabbing a few fries before tipping the bag toward me. I dig in, not shy about grabbing a handful.

"Best fries," I speak with my mouth full.

"So good." She hums with her eyes closed. There's nothing mindful or demure about the way she attacks her food. She's a hundred percent on that.

"One more stop but this one requires a bit of driving for the cake. Should we eat this stuff first?" Since we already established we have no boundary with food, I reach across the center console and steal a fry from the bag that is still on her lap. Then I circle the parking lot, parking in the back. She's not hesitant as she snacks, adding another fry as she chews the first one down. "So, I know you lost your camera, but other than that, how do you like your internship?"

She finished her fry before saying, "I like photography."

"Is that all?"

"And hockey."

"Fair enough." I reach into the bag from Red Barn and pullout a foil-wrapped kabob. I take a bite before I ask, "Do you have any questions for me?"

She pauses, not rushing her question, giving me just enough time to wonder whether I should have opened the floor for questions. "Why did you ask me to get food with you?"

"I was hungry." Easy question. Even if it's not the whole truth. I'm not going to say that ever since I first saw her, I can't stop thinking about her. *That* would be weird to say.

"Is that all?"

"Maybe I wanted to talk to you." I risk another side-eye, pulling my lips into a smirk.

We help ourselves to handfuls of fries. A pleased smile forms on her lips. "So, you say you procrastinate everything but hockey. What else do you do to procrastinate?"

"Good question." I scratch the top of my head, wondering if I should acknowledge the single biggest weight of pressure I feel every day. The pressure I get from Bill to do everything perfectly. "At the moment, basically anything but hockey."

"This is so good." She bleeps out a chuckle as she unwraps her own kabob. I struggle not to stare at how her lips turn up as if we'd just done something masterful. I keep my gaze locked on her as she smiles through each bite. With her hair over the shoulder like that, she looks like a model posing for a food commercial. It's the kind of beauty that exists only when a girl doesn't know she's pretty. I can't stop watching her. Before she catches me gazing at her, I say, "So, three restaurants; that's going to be our thing."

"Right," she says, her tone drenched in sarcasm. "Because we need a thing."

I raise an inquiring brow at her while I wad my empty wrapper into a ball and stuff it into the sack. "You just never know."

She follows my lead, rolling up her empty wrapper and stuffing it into the sack. "I'm full but we still have cheesecake waiting for us at the next place. Should I call to cancel it?"

"Oh no." I shift my car into gear and drive out. "We are in this together. No quitters."

"You're kidding." Her hand drops to her stomach. "I can't eat another bite. You have to remember I'm half your size. Maybe three restaurants works for you, but I'm going to be sick."

She's all talk.

There's no way anybody can resist the brownie explosion cheesecake when they see it.

When I get the final sack from JD's, I don't open it, and she holds it at bay, refusing to look at it, citing a belly ache. I exit the parking lot. "So, serious question. Since this cake has both brownie and cheesecake, if you could only have one, which one would it be?"

"You can't ask me that." She playfully frowns at me. "That's like asking who my favorite child is."

"It's not even close to the same thing. Plus, you don't have kids." A smirk tugs at the corners of my mouth, but I hold it back, pretending to be serious. "Cheesecake and brownies are renewables. Children are not. They are irreplaceable."

Surprise edges in her facial expression, and I can tell by the way her lips pinch together that she's holding back a rebuttal.

Or maybe I stumped her.

I arrive at the arena parking lot, and since there's only one car, I assume it's hers. She doesn't say it isn't when I pull up beside it and park. She starts to open her door, but I hand her the sack, and say, "Good thing it's both cheesecake and brownies. I won't make you choose."

"Nah." She pushes the bag back at me. "It's yours. You paid for it."

I hold a firm hand out toward her. "Save it for later when you are thinking about me."

"I would never—" She cuts herself off with an annoyed huff, but I push the sack farther out and she takes it, flashing a seriously flirty smile back at me. It's a smile she hasn't showed me yet, but I'm instantly addicted to it. I smile ear to ear when she shuts the door, thinking about how fun it is to make her smile.

At home, I find my mom's bedroom light on as I pass down the hall. Per the usual, I wait for her to call out, but to my surprise it's Bill's voice that breaks the silence first. "Noah, did practice run late?"

I stop and turn to their bedroom door. "Nope." I stare forward, not daring to make eye contact. This living arrangement is so complicated. My mom married Bill a day before I turned seventeen, after living as a single mom for my entire childhood. If I had it my way, I would have moved out on my own back then, but I'm not making enough. It's been a weird transition for me, but overall, it's been a relief to see my mom finally happy, finding someone who loves her. Oddly enough, I was the source that unknowingly brought them together. When Bill was scouting me, he accidentally—as he puts it—scouted my mom.

Maybe it's a dream come true to see my struggling mother marry a billionaire, but it's not without its issues. Bill offered me a spot on his hockey team, but he barely pays anything. I vowed to save what I made by staying here, but every day I regret this decision. It's too much of my professional life blending with my private life, and I'm going to need to find another source of income soon so I can move out or I'm going to end up leaving this team. Leaving the team would be ideal, especially if I can move up to the NHL, but it's not like I have offers waiting for me.

I wait, as I already know what Bill's getting at. He's an expert at meddling, and not just interfering, but negotiations where he ends up getting exactly what he wants. He's not a bad guy. That's not his deal at all. I appreciate everything he does for me. But sometimes I think he cares too much and doesn't know when he's overstepping a boundary. I've learned to refuse to offer any more information than what he asks for.

The news program they watch every night blares from the wall TV, but he speaks over the theme song. "Why are you home so late?"

"I, ah, stayed to help someone." I don't dare tell him another detail. I don't have a curfew, and I'm certainly not accountable to him.

"That's awfully nice of you," my mom adds, her voice sleepy as if she's been fighting going to sleep. Her blonde hair is tied back in a ponytail, and she fidgets with the end of it. She always looks happy when she's snuggled up to Bill, and I'm glad she has him. I don't have to worry about her anymore, but it's still so weird to see my mom married to my boss. I don't like to tell people I'm technically related to Bill, because I would hate the guys to think I receive favoritism, because trust me, I'm far from his favorite player.

"Say, about the charity banquet next week." Bill's overgrown salt-and-pepper eyebrows wag at me. "I was thinking you should ask Kaylee Bradworth."

I blink, recalling how this is how he gaslit me into asking Haileigh Goberson to the gala. I don't even like Haileigh, nor did I want to go to the gala. I find her high-pitched laugh to be the most annoying sound on the planet. Bill had insisted it was a great "connection" to make since her dad is a Mapleton city commissioner. "Ah, no thanks. I wasn't going to bring a date. It's just deep-fried turkey. I don't think any of the guys are bringing dates unless they have girlfriends or wives."

"Kaylee's dad is running for the Park and Recreation Board this year. He'd be a great connection to have." I am not one bit surprised this is his speech, and I struggle not to roll my eyes as he drones on. "Especially if you want to do any coaching or perhaps go into personal training after your AHL career ends. Really, anything with athletics."

Bill is all about working connections. I call it using people, but he says everyone uses everyone, which I think is disgusting. "I'm not bringing a date." I stride away from their door, calling back, "Night."

I didn't care either way about the date situation or Kaylee. She's a nice lady. We actually went to high school together. I'm sure we'd get along fine, but this is about me not wanting to be controlled by Bill. He's the kind of guy that once you give an inch, he takes a mile, and he always has these little schemes he's cooking up.

I want nothing to do with them.

No, thank you.

I pad down the hall, right as Bill's elderly bulldog wobbles out of my room with something in his mouth. You have to watch Puck because he makes a hobby out of exposing your most private possessions. Like the time he found Bill's private journal and decided to announce its existence to both our extended families right in the middle of Thanksgiving dinner. I laughed at that one. However, he then turned his detective skills on me and drug out my super-strength athlete's foot cream. I stopped laughing.

"What do you have?" I reach my hand below his mouth and wedge my fingers between his jaws. There's something trapped in there, and his jaw is clamped as tight as it will go. "Drop it," I demand, but he lifts a nostril toward me and growls.

Out of patience, I jab my finger further inside his mouth and proceed to yank out the object. Once I see what it is, I'm glad I did. I could have just saved his life.

My prescription anxiety meds.

"Don't steal these again." I pat his head in more of a disciplinary than friendly way. "You could have died if you ate these."

I swear he rolls his eyes and plods away, and I inhale a deep breath and clench the bottle in my fist. The only thing worse than a meddling Bill Baker is Bill Baker's meddling bulldog.

I seriously can't make up this drama.

Six

Paisley

Friday morning, I stand under the covered entryway of the Mapleton Arena, glaring at the Granite Ice bus. It's another blizzardy day here, with the wind whipping all over the parking lot. I pull my coat tighter around me, grateful I opted for my combat boots. Long Island gets cold, but not like this. I've been told this year has had an unusual amount of snow, but there is a valve in the clouds that is wide open and only knows how to dump mounds and mounds of snow.

To complicate this blizzard situation, it's travel day.

That's what the team calls it.

I'm   calling   it nightmare-in-a-white-bus-that-smells-like-rotten-gym-socks day.

Up until now, I've avoided traveling with the team as I was never invited. I don't think it's super common for Granite Ice to haul around reporters. However, there are only travel games left on the schedule, and I don't have even one incriminating photo for my spread. I was out of options, so I asked Bill if I could ride with the team. He didn't seem that enthusiastic, but it worked out that their full-time social media person couldn't make it, so there was an extra seat.

Which leads me back to this nightmare bus trip. I had my mind set on getting game photos, but I hadn't thought about actually sitting on the bus with these guys. I really want to skip this part. I could take my car, but the weather is getting bad, and I hate driving in storms. I scan along the bus windows, seeing most of the seats are already filled, and I regretfully force my feet to move forward because I can't give up now.

With my hands squeezed into fists, I raise my chin in the wind and march forward, wrinkling my nose as the diesel fumes saturate the air. It's four steps up, and I meet a bus driver with blue hair. Blue hair is not the "in" style by any means, but this lady looks cute with her short, pixie cut. I breeze past her, and my eyes widen as I stare down the center aisle.

I learned in grade school to never try to sit by anyone. People always save seats for their friends, and the humiliation of walking down the aisle to be turned down, again and again, is something that's been burned in my brain.

I will never do that again.

Instead, I take the least desirable seat, the one directly behind the blue-haired bus driver, and slouch, pulling my phone in front of my face as a shield of invisibility.

"Excuse me, miss," the driver hollers, turning her head a measure as if her neck is so stiff she can't risk turning it even ninety degrees. "You need to move back. That seat is reserved for the coaches."

"It's fine. I don't mind sharing." Dropping my gaze to my lap, I pick at my thumbnail and cringe at how embarrassing it is to be the girl sitting next to the coach. Yet, that scenario is better than the walk-of-shame down the center aisle.

"Ah, no, miss. There are two coaches coming and as you can see there's only two seats per bench." She hikes her thumb over her shoulder. "Head on back and find a seat."

My gaze cuts to the exit. This was a mistake. I slide one foot in the aisle, en route to the door. When the driver shifts the handle and closes the exit door, my expression freezes hard and my heart sinks.

I'm trapped.

A pig in the slaughterhouse.

I'm about to be bacon.

Unless I want to make a scene and beg her to open the door, my only option is to move back.

My heart hammers like a drum as I slowly pivot to face down the center aisle. Every seat is filled with either team staff or players chatting to each other. I inch back, straining my eyes, praying under my breath. *Please don't make me walk all the way down, and then back again.*

That's the worst.

With each row that I pass, the guys raise their eyes to stare at me but don't utter a word of invitation to sit. As I arrive at the halfway mark—the emergency exit door—sweat slaps on my back. I eye the door longingly and fight with every fiber of my being to not run out of it. This is high school all over again.

I mean, my internship is over soon, and I'll leave this little town and never come back. Nobody will ever remember me.

"Paisley." A familiar voice firmly beckons from my left, and I shift my eyes, wanting not to turn my head, but I already know.

Noah.

I'm so desperately trying to hate him because he's one of them, but hating him is getting harder and harder.

I slowly turn to him, and he's sitting next to Jackson Owen. I frown, but Noah stands, and says, "Why don't you sit here? I can move to the back with Axl."

A sigh slips from Jackson's lips, and he jolts to his feet. "I'll sit with Axl." I blink, and Jackson's already heading down the aisle. I'm cringing hard, but Noah has a full smile on as he waves me forward. "There, the seat is already warmed up."

My skin is practically burning as I drop onto the seat, keeping my gaze low. "You didn't have to do that," I mutter as I drop my purse off my shoulder, letting it hit my feet. Even the bus driver was waiting for me, and the bus suddenly shakes into gear, and we pull forward.

"I wanted to." Noah's eyes sparkle with gold flecks that brighten his face so much it frankly infuriates me. Why does he get to look hot when I'm struggling to just do life? I let out a low overwhelmed chuckle. This guy must have some GPS that is locked on my coordinates and always knows what I need.

It's getting old.

Possibly a little weird.

How is it even possible?

"Well, thanks for saving me, again," I mumble out, relief flooding my chest. I'm slowly coming to the realization that it's impossible to hate Noah. Trust me, I've been trying hard to keep my wall up while around him. Even though he wears a Granite Ice logo, he is not like the rest of the guys. He might actually, maybe, be a little nice.

Not to mention the most shocking turn of events from the other day—the dude sent me home with a whole slice of cheesecake that he paid for. It doesn't get better than free cheesecake.

He playfully taps his finger to his lips and lets out an indulgent sigh. "Well, you know, you're going to have to make it up to me."

My body is positioned forward, but I toss a helpless look in his direction. "Now what?"

"I'll let you know." He nods, adding a smug smirk. "Are you taking photos again?"

"That is the plan, although I already hate this plan," I say through gritted teeth, as I do my best to erase what just happened to me from my memory.

"You know what I like about you?" The casual way he offers to compliment me makes my spine straighten, and I stare at him with bated breath, praying this isn't a setup. "What?" My T is extra sharp as I wait.

"You're not like anyone else."

"Are you rubbing that in my face?" I turn my head at a suspicious angle as my cheeks fire on like an oven. I already know I don't fit in.

"No." He drops his hand to my arm, and a sonic boom rumbles through it, searing my flesh.

"It's not a bad thing. You just don't conform. I don't see anyone else walking about in all black clothes and combat boots. I've never met anyone like you before."

I stare at his hand on my arm while my esophagus malfunctions—which allows for an awkward pause. I could offer a rebuttal and tell him he's wrong, but instead, I glare at him. His smile is comfortable, not at all condescending.

He holds up his phone, switching the conversation. "Want to watch TikTok?"

"Sure." Our gazes synchronize on his phone as I do my best to drown out the neighboring whispers about me. It's not lost on me that, once again, Noah rescued me.

Okay, there's confirmation that I was maybe wrong, and he is nice. But that's clearly just Noah, and he's on the wrong team.

The rest of these guys are still horrid.

Standing in front of my seat behind the penalty box, my camera is positioned to capture anything that can happen. This is my favorite spot. I learned when I was a teenager that if I sit here, I can nonchalantly take selfies with the guys' backs.

It's sort of a weird obsession.

But it doesn't make me a bad person.

I'm supposed to be finding the photos that make these guys look bad, but I can't help but keep drawing my eyes back to Noah. He's been sitting on the bench most of the game, and I got twelve "selfies" with him mewing. He's an excellent mewer. Clearly, those selfies are going into my personal collection, which nobody shall ever see.

A time-out is called, and the Granite Ice team gathers around Coach Carlson for whatever genius words he has to say. I've eavesdropped on an awful lot of his speeches, and I usually zone out when Carlson speaks. He's generic. It's Bill Baker you want to lean in for, because he has all the gossip. I scan the packed arena, waiting for something interesting to catch my eye. My stomach growls, and I contemplate getting another bucket of popcorn, but I wasn't much of a fan of the first bucket. Their salt-to-butter ratio wasn't even close to average, with so much salt I had to get an extra drink refill to choke it down.

Scratch the popcorn idea.

In my peripheral vision, the players nod in agreement at whatever Carlson said, and they give knuckies in solidarity before they skate back out. Noah skates out on the ice with a fire in his eyes. I dutifully adjust my camera settings back to action mode.

The team's losing pain is so thick it's palpable in the air. I don't think they'll win another game this season, but I've never seen a team with more heart. That would be endearing if I wasn't trying to make them look bad.

The puck drops.

I do my best to use my phone to follow the action over the ice, hoping to get something worth saving. Axl is the best for controversy, because he gets in the most fights. Unfortunately, he's been keeping his temper in check, and he hangs back while Noah quickly takes control of the puck and streaks down the ice. He smokes past the defensemen and cuts toward the net. He's so nimble and fast, it's hard not to be amazed.

Noah has the talent to make me forget there is even a hockey game going on. I pull my gaze away from him for a second to scan the arena. All sets of eyes are glued on him as he puts on a fantastic show. Imagine just casually strolling by an ice rink and seeing him. Even people who have no idea what hockey is about would be stunned.

My gaze returns to Noah, and I follow him, snapping photos. When he gets to the front of the net, I rise to the tips of my toes in excitement, and I struggle to hold my phone steady. The crowd erupts in cheers as he shoots the puck, and it flies past the goalie and into the net! I snap a photo right as it goes in, getting both the goal and Noah in the shot.

That was easily the coolest thing to happen since I've been in Mapleton. Noah raises his fist in triumph, and his Granite Ice teammates swarm him. Seriously, somebody needs to tell Marvel about this guy. I don't need a photo of him looking this good for my spread, as this would destroy my plan, but it's an excellent shot. I'll just slip this one into my personal collection as well.

The scoreboard shows they are tied. For the first time in weeks, they have a real chance to win a game. They battle for the rest of the period, with nobody able to break the tie. My heart is in my throat. You'd think I'm rooting for them.

I'm clearly not.

It's the pressure to not miss anything.

As the clock winds down to the final seconds, Axl has the puck at center ice. He dodges a defenseman, skating along the boards and across the blueline. Another defenseman closes in on him, and Axl can't break free.

My eyes dart back to Noah.

He's open and in front of the net, but Axl has no clear path for a pass. I zoom my phone camera back on Axl. It would be nice if he would punch someone right about now. The guy used to be a goldmine for incriminating footage, but something has changed.

Instead of losing his temper, Axl maintains control of his attitude—and the puck—as he skates behind the net. Right as Noah skates in to assist, the defenseman slickly steals the puck and quickly fires a pass up the ice. The opposing center snatches the pass and takes off on a breakaway. He comes in on the goalie, makes a quick move, and fires the puck in the back of the net.

The crowd erupts in cheers.

I can't digest how fast that went. My stomach twists as my gaze flies to the clock. It shows only one second left. They take one final meaningless faceoff, and the final buzzer blares, signaling the end of the game. Nausea brews, and a deep sadness for the team sets in my heart. With heads hung low, the players skate off the ice.

I also feel defeated and let out a disgruntled sigh. All the shots I got were normal hockey shots, plus all the hot ones of Noah—which aren't going to help my assignment. I got nothing to prove my case that these guys should be hated. But as I drop my gaze, I start to feel like maybe that's okay.

They played hard.

It's not their fault that their boss is Bill Baker. Maybe I don't have to write a whole hit piece on them. I can write something normal that isn't that glowing. I stuff my phone in my pocket and head out with urgency, hoping to get on the bus before all the seats are taken. My efforts are rewarded. I'm the first one on the bus, and I plop down in the second row, taking the window seat.

A few minutes later, the team files onto the bus. I avoid eye contact as they seem to claim the same seats as before, and Noah plops down next to me as soon as he sees me. His Granite Ice beanie is pulled low, covering the bottom of his ears, the way he normally wears it. A flat frown of forlornity washes his normally happy expression clear off his face, and his gaze cuts to me as he adds a wireless earbud in each ear. With not so much as one uttered word, he closes his eyes and rests his head back in the seat. I instinctively know not to talk. Sometimes people just want to be quiet, and I'm totally fine not talking.

It's been a long day, and I'm exhausted. A yawn spirals from deep in my gut. I slowly open my mouth to let it out as I wrap my arms across my chest in a self-snuggle position and relax even more in my seat. Tension releases from my body as soon as I lean against the window and close my eyes. With another couple of deep breaths, I nod off into a peaceful slumber.

Until someone taps me on my shoulder. My lashes flutter, alerting me to the tapping, but my mind is so calm it pulls me back to sleep. A wispy stream of air, basked in notes of a cool ocean breeze, wafts under my nose. For the faintest of moments, I think I'm sleeping near the ocean. My body is warm and toasty, as I stay snuggled up.

This is seriously the best nap of my life.

Why would I stop it now?

More shoulder tapping.

That's so rude.

One eye opens methodically.

My head is resting against the sleeve of a cozy gray sweatshirt. So, not a window I thought I was sleeping on. I yank my other eye open to confirm my face is propped up against somebody—that smells amazing. So much so that I want to bury my nose further into this arm, but that would be weird. I do the opposite and raise my gaze up.

Noah is staring down at me, his lips pinched together as if he has a secret. "You finally woke up. A good thing too, because we're back in Mapleton."

"Ah." I slowly sit up straight, looking back at the window. The window is still there, plus what looks like a fresh drool stain I pretend not to see, but it glistens back at me. My cheeks heat as I reach out and give it a nice little pat to make sure.

Yep. Still nice and windowy.

My gaze slides back to Noah. Somehow, in my unconscious state of slumber, I scooted all the way over and snuggled up to him. My face heats steadily into a full broil. "Did I sleep on your arm?"

A chuckle leaks out of his mouth. "Yeah, the driver took a pretty hard right a while back, and you just rolled with it."

"I'm sorry." I flatten my hand on his arm like I had offended it. It's such a nice arm. Firm and steady, the perfect platform for resting against. "I had no idea." I fluster more, as I can't seem to stop staring at his perfect arm. "This isn't something I normally do." I risk eye contact, and his flirty gleam is strong out of the corner of his eye. "Why didn't you shove me off or, at the very least, wake me?"

Players start to muster into the center aisle and head off the bus, creating a bustle of noise. Noah speaks over the commotion, "You know how it goes." He tips his head down, pulling my gaze toward him. "You have to make it up to me."

"I thought I already owed you from before." My mind is still fogged by that ocean-breeze scent thing he has going on, and I scramble to find my overstuffed purse and stand, falling into step behind him.

"About that, I have a request for that one." He gives me a side-eye, but it's our turn to get off the bus, so he lumbers forward until we make it down the bus steps. Then he turns toward me and for no reason I can explain—except to be unfair—he feels it is necessary to look incredibly hot. Not that it should have even been more possible, but his jaw steels, his attention locking fully on me.

And again with the ocean breeze, dude.

It's like he has a tropical island floating above his head that sends off ocean-tainted waves right when I think I'm strong enough to resist that smile.

I'm not a groaner.

Except for maybe when I get the stomach flu, but you can't fault me for that. I fight with every ounce of my soul not to emit the cryptic-death noise that spun in my gut. Nothing good can come from him having any request while looking that fine.

"The team is going to Red Barn Kabobs," he continues. "Something to do to decompress. You should come."

"Yeah, I would be lying if I said that sounds like fun to me." I wobble from one leg to the other as everything about that makes me itch. "After the mosh-pit issue, I think I'll avoid crowds forever." I let my gaze wander to the cement. It's dark out, with only a few lampposts to light this huge parking lot. They create a perfect beam on him to cast a big broad shadow. I blush, feeling this warm gooey feeling I should *not* be having next to him, as I can't help but think even his shadow is hot.

Who on earth has a hot shadow?

I look over at my shadow. It's quite stout and wide, making me look like I've gained fifty pounds. That's not fair. How does he even win with shadows?

"That wasn't an ask." His smile turns smug, and I pause. He is serious. My heart slams against my ribcage. I get he's attractive, and I was fine with that when I hated him. Now that he's spent the week rescuing me, all my thoughts about him being arrogant have mysteriously disappeared. All I want to do is memorize the way the colors in his eyes dance between a healthy auburn all the way to an aged copper.

My stomach wobbles as I counter, "How about three restaurants instead?"

He stands firm and shakes his head. "I'm not taking no for an answer on this one. You just successfully completed your first trip with us, and you're one of us now."

One of them?

My whole body tenses as he looks back at me.

I can't be one of them!

They're my enemy.

But that was before Noah, who is staring down at me with one of those heart-stopping smiles. It feels like I'll go anywhere if it means I can stare at him. "I guess I can go for an hour or so."

"Sounds like a plan." He hangs onto the word plan as his smile lingers.

"Yeah," I echo, emotions clogging my throat. I feel like I'm on the edge of a cliff. I have the option to back away slowly and I'll be safe. Inching forward just a little might have some serious implications. Without double thinking about it, I slide my foot forward and follow him.

Seven

NOAH

I wanted her attention, so I asked for it.

Now, Paisley and I straddle two of the last empty bar stools at Red Barn Kabobs. She knows everyone's names. If she is nervous, she doesn't show it, because she keeps talking to everyone.

I never noticed it before, as we'd only ever chatted about food and photos, but, man, she has hockey stats filed in her brain like a hockey Google machine.

NHL, AHL, college, and even high schools. I would never admit it to anyone, but I'm relieved when the subject finally goes somewhere other than hockey. "Hey, I saw the strangest thing." She slides to the edge of her seat, bouncing her gaze from Axl to Sophie to me.

"A skibbity toilet rizzlier Ohio," Axl interjects from across the table.

Sophie elbows him with a chuckle. "Sorry, he's been spending too much time with my little brother."

"No." Paisley wags her head, the seriousness in her expression making her eyes grow wide. "This morning when I was driving over to the arena, it was still a little dark out, and right as I pulled off the interstate, I glanced to the left—you know, where there's all those trees—and I swear I saw a monkey."

"You're not wrong. Mapleton has monkeys." Sophie juts to a more upright seating position and extends her hand in excitement. "I see them all the time!"

"So, this is a thing?" Paisley's gaze slides to me. "I thought I might be dreaming."

I nod. "Yeah, they are escaped circus monkeys, and Mapleton is famous for them."

"That's a little weird." Paisley shakes her head in bewilderment, her gaze directed at me. "I know I'm supposed to stick to sports, but I might have to add something about that to my article."

"Do it." I bark a supportive laugh. "You'll get so much more talk about it."

"You two are so cute together." Sophie wags a finger between us, and then, in a voice as loud as a stage whisper, says, "You are dating, right?"

"Nah—" Paisley starts to speak, but her feeble attempt at a rebuttal is over spoken by Sophie.

"I have the best idea! You both should join us on our couples' ski weekend!" Sophie's voice grows louder, and her focus slams back to Axl.

Axl picks up her idea and rushes to expound. "Yeah, Sophie booked this all-inclusive ski package at Mapleton's ski lodge. We have a cabin, ski rentals, and lift tickets. We have extra tickets because Jackson and his lady friend were going to go, but they broke it off. You should come up. Everything's already paid for. You'd be doing a favor to not waste them."

I level my gaze with Paisley's. We pause for a long moment, as if we are both yielding to the other. She seems as stunned as I am.

Here we are—Paisley and I—sitting together on something that looks like a date, but I don't want to make her uncomfortable by insinuating things that aren't real.

We're definitely not a couple.

We will not be going on any couples' weekends.

Even though I love snowboarding.

The team doesn't have a hockey game this weekend, which means that if I have no plans, I'll be hanging out at the house with my mom and Bill.

I would love a weekend away from Bill.

Paisley's gaze is locked on mine with no indication that I should refuse this gift.

Hmm, would it be wrong to insinuate a little?

For the sake of snowboarding.

It wouldn't feel wrong.

It feels like fun.

Paisley still hasn't uttered a word. She's sitting on her stool, the muted-yellow bar light looming over her, lighting her best side.

Who am I kidding?

All her sides are the best ones.

I'm looking for a secret wink to let me know she likes free stuff, too, but she's still. I finally reply for us both. "It's sort of new . . ." I ease my words to not give away any embellishment. A light pink fires across the tops of Paisley's cheeks. I tip my head toward her. "I love snowboarding. What do you think? Should we join them in their already-paid-for-couples' skiing weekend?"

"Er, thank you so much for thinking of us." She clears her throat and continues with a non-answer, "That's certainly generous."

I can already feel the wind in my face as I fly down the slopes. My adrenaline pumps as I lean closer, wagging my brows. "We don't have a game, so you're also off. I don't think it's an offer we should refuse."

Her muteness carries on for a beat longer than what feels comfortable before she leans into me, sending waves of her effervescent sweet scent and smiling coyly at me. An electric zap spirals through my body, and it's still zapping when she says, "I would love a couples' getaway. After all, this weekend is Valentine's Day."

"Oh, really?" I startle. The word Valentine echoes in my head so loudly that I start seeing a mirage of red hearts and stuffed teddy bears. Sweat beads on my brow as I realize that the stakes are suddenly raised.

Why am I the last one to find this out?

Valentine's weekends are for serious couples.

Not just people who want to get free ski passes.

I'd look like a complete jerk backing out now. I press my teeth into my lip, not enough to hurt but enough for me to feel the sting. "That sounds like, ah, such a great p-plan."

"Right!" Sophie's tone ticks up a notch. "We can all ride together. It's going to be epic."

My gaze replants on Paisley. Her complexion has gone ashen as she swings her bar stool back and forth. Her straight expression is silently hinting she might need to talk about this.

"Well, it's getting late." I stretch my arms wide, pretending I'm not in a hurry to get away from these two before I agree to do something else—like a Vegas trip to get married. I casually look at Paisley, pleading with my eyes. "You want me to take you home?"

"We can get out of here." She nods as she slides off her stool and slips on her coat.

I stand, placing a protective hand on her lower back as I stride a half step behind her. We are about a yard away from the table before she leans in and harshly whispers, "What were you thinking back there?"

"I know!" I slam my gaze to the ceiling. "I was hung up on the free skiing. I didn't realize it was a romantic couples thing."

We continue to pace away from the table at a brisk speed. Paisley hisses under her breath, "Sophie flat out said couples' weekend when she offered."

I open the exit door and wait for her to pass through it. "Right, but nobody gave me a heads-up about the Valentine's thing. Where did that come from?"

"It came from the calendar." She snicker-laughs.

I drop my voice to include more calm inflections. "It's fine, really. Just because it's a couples' thing doesn't mean we can't enjoy the free skiing. It doesn't change anything because a pink angel in a diaper claimed this weekend."

Her expression flattens, and the only clue to how she's feeling are her round, now vulnerable eyes. "You still want to go knowing it's Valentine's Day?"

"We are both off work and don't have to make a big deal about the couple things. It's free skiing."

"Right." Her arms cross over her chest, as we are almost to my car. She echoes as if she's still trying to convince herself. "Just free skiing."

"And maybe some hot chocolate." I gesture toward her, hoping to lighten the mood. "Nothing wrong with that."

"Hot chocolate is good." Her chin raises and lowers. "And probably a lot of time with Sophie and Axl, which will be great. It will give me a chance to get to know them better." Her inflections have calmed down now. I risk direct eye contact as I'm no longer afraid her angered gaze is going to disintegrate me.

"Right. Don't worry." I open my door and get in. I'm calm on the outside, but my brain is still flashing a mirage of chocolate candy hearts, red roses, and cards with images of couples dancing and kissing. The brain filter that I should have put in place falters, and I word vomit the thoughts that should have stayed silent. "It'll be totally fine. It's not like there'll be any kissing or anything."

"Wait. What?" She opens her door with urgency and slides in next to me, her eyes searching for answers in mine. "Why would you blurt that out?"

My gaze slams to the heavens.

Why would I blurt that out?

For real, Noah.

"It was a joke?" My defense sounds like a question, and I avoid her gaze as I start the car and pull forward, so ready to change this subject. "Anyway, about those wild monkeys . . ."

When I get home, I dump the contents of my travel bag on my bed and sort through them. Unused socks. I drop them back into the bag, as I will definitely need them for snowboarding. Wireless earbuds. Yep, back in the bag those go, because Axl has been known to snore. The rest of the stuff is dirty laundry, so I scoop that all up in one giant heap and walk it over to my hamper. I'll have to deal with that when I get back.

I cross my room again to my closet and open the door right as my mom pops her head in. "Hey, I thought you were done with overnight travel games?" Her reading glasses are on the tip of her nose, indicating that she's already taken out her contacts for the night and is passing on her way to bed to watch the news with Bill.

"We are." I snatch a Granite Ice sweatshirt off the hanger and roll it up as I walk back to my bed. "I got invited to go snowboarding this weekend with Axl and his fiancé. We are leaving in the morning."

"Oh, Sophie." She nods, the ends of her lips pulling into a pleased grin. "That sounds like fun. Is it just the three of you going?"

"Nope." I roll my lips in and silently chew myself out for not moving out of my parents' house sooner. I love my mom dearly, but it's moments like this that drive me insane. I have no idea what this little trip with Paisley means, but I know my mom's going to insist she needs to know what it means. "And Paisley."

"Paisley?" On cue, one eyebrow pitches up in the form of an actual question mark. I'm not even exaggerating. It has an arch and a squiggle, and it's asking me to expound.

I stare forward, racking my brain to answer her eyebrow. "I don't think I know her last name." I draw a blank as I recall our past conversations. "It never came up."

"Hmm. Interesting." Her lips even into a straight line. I'm almost off the hook, as I can see her brow lowering, but then the worst thing ever happens.

Bill walks up and parks a hand on my doorframe. "What's interesting?"

The only thing worse than living with your mom as an adult is also living with your boss. Why didn't I close and lock the door when I had the chance? I flick my attention to my bag, doing my best to not welcome more questions. "I'm going skiing this weekend with Axl and Sophie."

"And Paisley." Mom aims her question-mark eyebrow at Bill like I'm fourteen and this is my first date.

"Paisley." Bill's gaze cuts to me. Cue the interrogation in three, two—"Why does that name sound familiar?"

"She's been working with the team for a few weeks." I keep the comments focused on her professional life. "You hired her for PR."

"I didn't hire anyone." His deer-in-the-headlights look flashes. "Oh, her! Yeah, she's not my employee. She's working for some magazine, and she's here for a little over a month."

"Right."

"I'm glad you brought her up." His hand drops off my doorframe, and he takes several long, unwelcome steps into the room. "Do you sense something is off about her?"

"Like what?" My T is extra sharp to send the strong hint that I really don't care to discuss this with him.

"I don't know." He lifts his hand and scratches the middle of the bald spot on his head with his pointer finger. "I can't place it, but something is strange about the way she's always lurking around, taking photos—"

"Because that's her job." What is he even getting at? I grab another sweatshirt from my closet and some snow pants and stuff them into my bag.

Bill hums for a beat before adding, "Anyway, about Kaylee Bradworth."

Disbelief floods my whole body, and I spin on my heel and face Bill. "What about her?"

"I invited her to the charity banquet to sit by us."

I struggle not to scream at the top of my lungs, and somehow, miraculously I speak with an even tone. "Why would you do that?"

"You said you weren't going to bring a date, and we had the seating. I didn't want to miss an opportunity to get to know someone."

"You are—"

"An excellent matchmaker." His smug smile fills in.

"That's not at all what I was about to say." I lower my gaze to the floor and focus on deep steady breaths. I'm going to have to increase my anxiety medication dosage if I continue to live with Bill much longer.

"It's true. Just ask Sophie and Axl." Pride shines through his expression. "They seem to be exceptionally happy."

I can't listen to this anymore.

I certainly can't go on setups with Kaylee Bradbury or Bradworth or whatever her name is.

Not when I have my own . . .

My . . .

Paisley isn't anything but a friend, but it matters because it's my life. I make the decisions about my life. Not Bill Baker. I seriously need to look for an apartment as soon as I get back from this trip. Jotting that down in my inner to-do list.

"So, ah, be there by six for social hour, and maybe try some of my Old Spice I have in the bathroom." His thumb angles behind him toward his bathroom and I cringe.

"I'm not using your cologne," I grumble.

"The ladies love it." His gaze slides to my mom. "Right, honey?"

"He's not lying." She smiles back, and all I want to do is melt into the floor. Again, I'm happy my mom is finally happy, but I can't hear this.

"Stop." I exaggeratedly place my hands over my ears.

"Fine." Bill wraps an arm around my mom's waist, both beaming out giant smiles. He holds up a finger with his free hand. "And tell me what this Paisley's last name is. We need to know more about her."

"You're the one who gave her an office," I grumble. "Maybe you should have asked her?"

"That's right. I must have written it down somewhere." His brows furrow together. "I'll have to do some digging."

I let out an exasperated sigh. "What does it matter to you what her last name is?"

"Noah, we need to figure out who she really is." Bill aims the most cryptic expression at me. "She might be a Palmer City Voltage fan, and we *can't* have that."

"I don't know what you have against them." I almost stutter at his ridiculousness. "We rarely even play them. They are in a different conference."

"You're right." Bill wags his head, his lips rolling in tightly. "But I went to their games for years when I lived in Colorado. They win too much, especially for a team in such a small town. They have to be cheating, and if they aren't, it's just annoying."

"We are a team in a small town."

"It's different," he quips back. "Plus, they think they are so cool. Did you see what their owner did? He got them one of those fancy lightning machines, just like Tampa has." He throws his head back, disgust oozing out of his expression. "Like, come on. What a showoff."

I bite back a smirk, knowing full well that Bill is more jealous than anything. Now that he's voiced what he's jealous of, I can fully visualize Bill getting a lightning machine sometime soon. "Yeah, okay. I guess I'll make sure to ask Paisley if she's a Voltage fan."

"Alright, honey." My mom reaches out and gives me a side hug. "I'm headed to bed, but you have a nice trip."

They finally leave my room and I turn back to my bag, doing a final scan. The only thing that's missing are my anxiety meds. I slide my gaze back to my nightstand, and they are gone. Again.

Puck.

That stubborn dog.

I heave a heavy sigh. My anxiety ticks up thinking about how high my anxiety will be if I don't have my meds, and I hurry down the hall. My mom's door is already closed, and I don't stop to knock, because they never let Puck sleep in there. Usually, he sleeps by the kitchen backdoor, and I scurry through the hall, and down the back staircase.

He's right where I thought he'd be—sitting next to the door. One eye is closed, and the other eye is on the fridge as he patiently waits for Bill to come down for his midnight snack. He has everyone's eating times memorized, and he doesn't miss an opportunity to graze.

"Hey, Puck," I whisper shout. "What's in your mouth?" I drop to the floor in front of him, one palm on the marble floor, while the other hand digs into the side of his clenched teeth. His jaw snaps open, but nothing falls out. "Where are my meds?" I ask with a light-hearted teasing voice as I understand this is now a game he's playing. "Did you hide them?"

He juts out his tongue, points his ears back, and smiles at me while wagging his stumpy tail.

"Okay, that's fine if you want to play, but the games are over. I'm leaving town tomorrow, and I need them. Where did you put them?"

More tail wagging.

I swipe a hand through my hair. I can't believe this is happening. I'm clearly stupid for not leaving the pills locked in the medicine cabinet. I used to do that, but there were so many days I would forget to take them. One time in particular was before a game, and I had a full-fledged panic attack while I was on the ice. My chest tightened and I couldn't breathe. After that happened, I vowed to always keep them by my bed, so it is the first thing I see in the morning.

I'll have to call my doctor in the morning to see if he can send a replacement prescription over to the pharmacy, but tomorrow is

Saturday, and we are leaving early. He's more than likely not going to be in until Monday.

My gaze drops to the side, as I overthink this, because that's what I do.

It might be okay if I skip them for the weekend. It's not like we are going to be doing anything stressful. I mainly need them for games. Yeah. I spin on my heel and head back upstairs to get some sleep. It's not a big deal. I'll get more on Monday when we are back in town.

Eight

Paisley

Sophie: We are just pulling into the Arena. Look for the black Ford Lincoln Navigator.

I'm sitting in my car, staring at my phone, and reading the text. The sun isn't even up yet, and it's way too early to solve riddles.

Me: Do you mean Lincoln Navigator?

Before she can reply, a black Navigator with tinted windows rolls to a stop in front of me. I check the emblem on the hood. It's Lincoln, with dealer plates. Chuckling, I get out of my car, cross the parking lot to the SUV, and open the back door. Axl is driving, with Sophie riding shotgun. I throw my small backpack on the floor and climb inside. "Morning."

"Morning," Sophie calls back. "Obviously, we are still waiting on Noah. He said he's running late."

"Oh, that's okay." I pause for a moment, wondering why he never texted me. "So, did you get a new Navigator?"

"No, it's a Ford Lincoln Navigator, and it's not mine. Just a rental. I wanted something with third-row seating for all the extra bags, so we'd be comfortable." Sophie smiles brightly, not understanding why I'm confused—or rather why *she is confused.*

"I get that Ford owns Lincoln, but I think this make is just called Lincoln." My gaze cuts to Axl, who is wearing an amused grin in the reflection of the rearview mirror.

"Don't even bother trying to explain it to her. Since the dealership had the sign that said both, she insists this is what it is," he says when he catches me staring at him. "I lost ten minutes of my life I'll never get back."

"Got it." I nod, and Noah's SUV pulls in next to us, parking at a bit of a slant. Instead of straightening his car to fit between the painted lines, he jumps out and rushes over, opening the back hatch to drop a bag in. Then he runs over to his door and pants as if he's out of breath. "Hey, sorry I'm late. My dog took my . . . ah, vitamins last night, and I was a little worried he might eat them. I didn't want him to get sick, so I tried looking again this morning."

"You keep us waiting and lead with 'the dog ate my' excuse," Axl replies. "Can't you come up with something better than that?"

"I didn't say he ate them. He hides things sometimes. But yeah, I'm worried he might eat them." He slides in next to me and shuts his door. Axl pulls the vehicle forward and steers toward the road. Noah allows himself a moment to breathe. His chest seems to relax, and he looks over at me. "Morning. How is your day going?"

I'm quieter than normal when I reply, "Better than yours."

Axl chimes in, his voice not concealing the cackle of laughter he's desperately holding back. "Are you ready to ride in Sophie's new Ford Lincoln Navigator?"

"What? I don't understand the joke." Noah looks at him, and then cuts a gaze at Sophie. "Isn't this a Navigator?"

Axl's shoulders visibly bounce, but he's tough and doesn't leak out even a snicker. "Don't bother explaining it."

"I'm confused." Noah looks back at me.

"So are the rest of us." I resist an audible laugh, as I hate to make fun of people, even though it is in good fun.

"Okay then." Noah leans back in his seat and proceeds to tap his foot.

"So, Paisley," Sophie says, steering the conversation in a new direction, "I'm excited you could make it. The guys go everywhere together. I'm glad to have another female along to even it out."

"Oh, yeah, before I forget." Noah leans in, a teasing gleam sparking out of his eye. "Bill needs to make sure you aren't a Palmer City Voltage fan."

"The Voltage?" I give him a side-eye, and my body stiffens as I have no idea where this is coming from. "No, I can't say I am. I don't have anything against them, though."

"You're dating this girl, and you don't even know what her favorite hockey team is?" Axl heckles.

"I said we are newish," Noah quips back, but his gaze lingers on me. "Of course, her favorite team is Granite Ice."

"You guys are certainly wearing off on me." My lips pull into a squeamish smile as all I can think about is how I first came to

Mapleton to destroy this team. Now they are welcoming me on an all-paid-for trip. What would they say if they knew what I was originally up to? I resist the urge to hang my head because that would be all too telling of my shame. My fingernail finds its way between my teeth. I nibble at it, so much guilt washing over me.

I can't change the reason I came here.

I also am not going to not live my life, hiding in shame.

I argue with myself that it's in the past. I can't change it, and I might as well move on from it and enjoy the trip.

"Do you guys want to watch a movie?" Sophie calls back, while handing a remote to me. "In the spirit of Valentine's weekend, I grabbed every single romcom I have."

"Great." Axl groans out. "Glad I'm driving."

My gaze shifts to Noah, and he's untriggered. "Are you watching or sleeping?"

"I just woke up. I don't need a nap." He crosses his arms over his chest, as if he's preparing to sit a while. "I'll watch it with you."

I settle in, pulling a leg under me into a more comfortable position. I turn my attention to the screen in front of my seat, and I turn it on with the remote. Some previews flash on and I try to pay attention. It only takes a moment, and my gaze slides back to Noah. I remember how I accidentally snuggled with his arm on our last road trip. Warm feelings return, and I can't help but wish we could scoot a little closer as the movie previews roll.

His leg is doing that restless leg thing, but he's tuned into the screen.

Axl gets on the interstate, and I'm overwhelmed with the feeling of belonging. Everyone is treating me like we're a friend group, and it's oddly emotional since I've never really had this before. I try to get into the movie but as soon as it's quiet the niggling in the back of my head says I should be ashamed to even go on this trip after all I did to hurt these guys. My brow bends down, as I don't know why this is bothering me so much now. I'm supposed to be having fun. Everyone is joking and laughing, and I can't shake the feeling that this is a terrible idea to go on this trip. As much as I want to have friends, I don't deserve to have these guys as friends. Chewing on my thumbnail again, I force my attention to the movie, and I tell myself repeatedly that it's only one night, and I leave Mapleton next week. It can't be that bad . . .

With the sun in full bloom over the mountains, we arrive at the ski resort less than an hour later. The air is brisk, springing me wide awake as we plow through the new snow, skis and poles in hand, and we pause to gear up.

Sophie and the guys all grab snowboards and seem to flawlessly slip into their brand-name ski goggles. Axl and Sophie glide over the snow, heading out to the lift. I'm the only one who struggles to remember how to snap my boot shut. It takes me a few tries of jabbing my toe into the binding and leaning all my weight back until I hear the heel click. "Finally." I look up, and Noah is waiting. "Sorry it took so long."

"It's not a race. We're here all day." He pushes off with his free foot to slide over the snow toward the lift. I follow behind, shuffling my feet forward, but can't seem to get moving. The packed snow beneath the powder proves slippery, and I'm stuck in one place.

"Try bending your knees," Noah calls back from up ahead, where he pauses again to wait on me.

I feel like a penguin as I shift my weight from one ski to the next. There's no way I even remotely look like I know what I'm doing. Laughter spirals in my gut as I ski-waddle on. "Sorry, it's been years since I skied. I don't remember it being this hard to get going."

"It's okay. It's easier on the hill." His brows dip together, nearly joining in the middle. "They went to the black diamonds. Maybe we should try a green?"

"Oh, no." I almost scowl at the mere suggestion that I must start on the bunny slopes. I jab my poles into the snow to push myself forward. That helps the most, and I ski-waddle, pole-slide over until I'm finally next to him. "I can ski just fine. It's this flat earth stuff that's got me stuck."

"Are you sure?"

"Yes."

"Okay, then." He nods toward the lift, but his gaze stays locked on me, as if he's daring me. "This is our ride. It's an express to the top."

"That sounds perfect." I shuffle forward until I'm between the ropes.

He gives me a bit of a suspicious side-eye. "Do you remember how to get on a lift?"

"You just sit, right?" I eye the pairs of people already riding the lift, and it's as simple as I remember it. The duo in front of us positions themselves in the line, and a chair comes up behind them, scooping them up. Now it's our turn. I dig my poles into the snow and steadily push myself forward. The last thing I need to do is get beamed in the back with a ski chair. I make it to my spot just in time. The chair nudges at the back of my calves, and Noah and I sit, and take off for the sky.

This lift is faster than any lift I've ever ridden. In no time we are above the trees. Noah elbows me on purpose, speaking through a snicker. "Something tells me you are pretending to be a novice so you can blow dust at me as soon as we are at the top."

"Nope." I shake my head, laughing too. "That is not my plan. I've skied some, but not since middle school, and clearly, I forgot everything I thought I knew."

"Oh, yes." His head rolls back into the start of a nod. "I forgot. You always have a plan. What is it this time?"

"It's just the basic plan." I offer a teasing smile, even though my gut is feeling a little loopy from the chairlift swaying. "It includes not dying. Not hitting a tree. Not getting lost. Not ending up being the subject of one of those made-for-TV movies where some chick gets sucked into an avalanche and survives for three days while the whole town searches for her, and in the end is rescued by an adorable Husky."

"Basic plans are so boring. They only focus on the bad things. You need to upgrade to the platinum plan. That's where the good stuff happens."

His tone is laced with so much flirtation, I can't help but bat my lashes. "Do tell of this platinum plan."

"Well, for starters, you could have fun." He elbows me lightly and tacks on, "Or you might get to snuggle on the ski lift with a handsome date."

"We aren't snuggling." I dart my eyes to the sliver of space that's left between our bodies. It's small but totally there—not that it would be bad to snuggle.

Would it be bad?

Heat rises to my face as I manage to reply, "We aren't even touching at the hips."

"Right, but that's because you bought into the basic plan." He wags his brows at me. "You need to think about upgrading the plan."

"I do." My voice is flat, concealing all hints that my heart is hammering in my chest. Everything about this flirty side of Noah makes me extremely aware of the fact we only have a tiny sliver of space separating our bodies.

"You do." I wait for him to do a flirty look away, but he doesn't even blink. His eyes hold mine in a way that's more daring than friendly. I know what I'm doing. Two can play this game. I scoot closer to him, closing the gap between us, silently challenging him to read between the lines.

Nowhere on any planet does me being interested in Noah Miller make any sense. However, we are technically not rooted on the planet now—we are floating through the sky. So all my racing thoughts are totally fine.

Like how I want to know what it feels like to have his arms wrapped around me so badly, that I feel like I'm about to suffocate over here on my side of the ski lift without it. Clearly, it's his fault because he's the one who suggested snuggling in the first place. My body seems to sway, inching even closer to him as I hold my breath and wait for a cue from him to lean even closer.

He wears a mischievous grin as his gaze shifts down to my lips. A hurricane of spirals erupts in my gut but then ends abruptly when our lift jolts and noticeably slows, cresting to the top of the hill. I regretfully pull my attention from him to gather my poles in one hand and get ready to stand. A brittle laugh fueled only by nerves leaks from my gut. "Here we go."

"On three." He counts down at the perfect tempo so that as soon as he says three, we both stand to glide forward to clear the way.

I drop a giant sigh of relief that I didn't fall, and I celebrate with a beaming smile. "Made it this far."

He lowers his goggles, adjusting the straps to fit perfectly underneath his beanie. He looks like a professional. I take the regular sunglasses out of my puffer coat pocket, slip them on, and pretend to feel confident.

"If it's okay," he says while he straps in his other boot to his snowboard, "I'll stay by you on this run until I know you got the hang of it."

"Yeah." I waddle-ski, pole-slide over to the side, mapping my path. The middle of the run looks the steepest with a big ditch that has huge dips. The side is banked and doesn't drop as fast. "Like I said before . . ." I inch toward the side and toss a look back at him to reassure him I know what I'm doing. "I was struggling because it was flat. Once I get on the slopes—"

It starts with a slip and a giant gust of wind.

Who turned on the wind?

My eyes pop open.

And I'm gone.

Whooooosh!

My knees lock with skis parallel and pointing straight ahead. I'm frozen in complete fear and can't remember how to cut or even if I ever knew how. I'm blazing down, smoking past even the most expert skiers, who know how to slow their descent. The run dips and then rises into tiny ramps that shoot me out even faster, and I wail out a scream at the top of my lungs.

How I haven't died yet is a miracle. Somehow, I'm still upright, and racing forward. Something crazy happens. I finally stop screaming to inhale a deep breath. I just survived one of the biggest drops on this run. A smile tugs on the corner of my mouth, and I inhale again. I slowly bend my knees and narrow my stance, shifting my weight to cut, and my legs start to shake.

Ka blam wham!

I'm suddenly back flippin' and belling floppin' like a flapjack in a truck stop diner, all the way down the hill. There's a yelp and a yip, and a long groan. One pole goes west, the other east. My skis snap out of my boots. I can't even begin to describe the assortment of leg splits I'm twisted into before I finally roll to a moaning stop. The cold seeps through my pants and inches deeper through my extremities. The wildest thing of all is that I'm not scared. I don't even flinch as I sprawl out in my snow-angel pose. I've connected the pattern, and I know Noah will rescue me.

It's what he does.

It's like fate, but handier.

"Paisley." The slicing of his snowboard tips me off that he's near me. Another second later, he cuts to a stop next to me, carrying both skis I had lost. "Are you trying to die today?"

No, that wasn't my plan at all. If I had it my way, we'd be riding that ski lift around all day, snuggling . . .

As I move to look at him, my shoulder pulsates rays of pain that shoot all the way down to my hip. I peel my body off the ground to sit up and carefully steady my boots in the snow to stand, asserting my best independent-woman tone. "I accidentally on purpose ran a, ah, test."

"Test?" he sputters out, his lips pinching into an amused smirk. "Any test that looks like that is clearly a failure."

"Not quite." I wag my finger at him to buy time, but it hurts to even move my finger. I'm not sure how I'm going to talk myself out of this one. "It was a test to see if you were, ah, in fact, telling the truth about staying with me."

"A lie-detector test, then?" His lips tug into a teasing smile as he passes my skis back over. "I clearly passed."

"Yes." I don't try to nod because I can already tell doing so would strengthen this pull that I have in my shoulder.

"Are you going to be able to make it down the hill?"

I dig my teeth in my bottom lip and stare at the ski lodge at the bottom of the hill. Even though I'd flown down half of the hill, there's still a nice jaunt to the bottom.

Not going to lie.

With the way my shoulder is throbbing, if I had the option to sit this out, I would. I don't have a thing to prove to myself. My gut rolls into a tight ball confirming I actually hate skiing.

"Tell you what," Noah says slowly, "you make it to the bottom, and I'll buy you a hot chocolate."

"Oh, yes." I nod, not feeling even the slightest bit better. "The hot chocolate you forewarned about with the kissing."

"Wow, that's certainly forward of you to suggest kissing, but only if it will make you feel better." He nods toward the ski lodge—that's still a long way down the hill. It looks like a Lego house from up here. "You first."

I wasn't nervous before because I was delusional. Clearly my memories of skiing in my younger years do not match up to my reality. I don't remember it being that hard. Now that I've discovered I have no natural balance, my nerves fire on. My legs are jittering when I step into my skis again, but I know I must do this.

It's too far to climb up.

And I have to get down somehow.

I swallow, fixing my gaze on the little Lego ski lodge.

"Come on." He waves me forward. "I'll be right behind you.

"If you say so." I breathe slowly, and shift my weight to one ski, allowing it to angle down. I take a minute to make sure the straps on the poles are around my wrist. I can't find a comfortable position to hold my left pole in because everywhere I try, it makes my shoulder pulsate.

Regretfully, I slowly push off. Not because I want to. I have no other choice. As soon as I start descending, I bend my knees and focus on balancing as I cut to turn the other way, and it works.

I'm not the fastest person out here anymore. My legs are working mostly okay, except for the shaking coming from my knees. That's straight fear. My shoulder seems to have lost most of its range of motion, and it throbs in pain, but I focus on the little Lego ski lodge down below as motivation to get me through this run.

Somehow, we manage to glide to a smooth stop at the lodge, where I whip off my beanie and sunglasses and drop an explosive sigh of relief. "I'm not going back up there."

"Nobody said you had to." Noah's grin is easy as he unlatches his boots and kicks up his board to prop it against the side of the lodge with the rest of the stored gear.

Despite the winter temps, I'm drenched in sweat and breathe heavily as we pass through the doors. I manage to hobble up the single set of stairs to the restaurant. Two hot chocolates later, we stroll back through the lodge in search of a spot to rest. All the tables are taken, and the only available seat is an oversized leather loveseat. A pile of children's books and a few discarded toys scatter over the corner, and it takes everything I have not to get up to tidy it up. Normally, my mind doesn't rest around clutter, but today I don't care. On a day with fewer bruises, I wouldn't be able to resist. "After you." Noah gestures toward the sofa.

"Don't mind if I do." The grunt is all mine. I plop down, propping my feet up on the little rustic coffee table. My body melts into the leather like it's chocolate at the beach.

His snicker laugh is instant, and his direct gaze warns me that he will force me to converse rather than rest in silence. "That smile says you're done skiing for the day."

"I can't say skiing is my forte." Now that I know my funeral is averted for at least another day, a chuckle moves inside me as I check my smartwatch. "It only took me an hour to almost die today. Not too bad." I bob my head, feeling the self-deprivation kick in. "If you're worried about me, I'm fine sitting here. You go ahead and get back out." I gesture out the window at all the happy skiers buzzing down the hill.

"I would rather sit here with you." He nudges his shoulder next to mine—thank goodness it's my good shoulder or I might have yelped. He effortlessly slouches into the cushions to match me.

"Consider that my gift to you." I take a sip of tepid hot chocolate, hoping to wash away at least some of my embarrassment. When I swallow, my cocoa-coated taste buds beg me to lean my head back, and my eyes close as almost every ligament in my body throbs in pain.

"You might consider getting checked out by a chiropractor or physician," Noah's voice cuts through my hazy thoughts. When I don't reply, he proceeds to pat my thigh, at which point my brain literally booms. "Hey, did you hear me? You might need a doctor."

My brain is still booming. I've never been one for public affection of any kind, but it's those soft little touches that always get me. Like, melt me even faster into this couch. I open one eye. Noah has a look of concern pinned on his brows, but my skin is begging for those snuggles he teased earlier.

"I'll be fine." Taking his cue, I reach over and pat his leg. "But thanks for your concern."

"I'm not trying to sound like a know-it-all, but I've seen an awful lot of injuries, and your whole shoulder looks completely disjointed. How you aren't screaming in pain is beyond me."

"Now that you mention it." I lean forward and proceed to run my hand along the top of my shoulder, checking for anything that feels weird, even though I have no idea what I'm feeling for. "I do feel a little lopsided." I downplay the intensity of the pain, but I can't deny something is a little off.

"Here." He reaches for my shoulder, and I immediately tense, jerk back, and yelp like one of those yippy dogs. "See, you are out of place." His tone is cautionary as he slides his hand over my shoulder blade.

"I'm fine." I blink at him, as if moving my eyelids proves my shoulder is functional.

He slides to the edge of the couch. "Come on. You need to be seen by a medical professional, and you're in luck, because the clinic takes walk-ins until noon. If we leave now, we'll have enough time to get there."

"I'm fine," I assert again, this time tossing my hair back over my shoulder, but the mere circular motion of my head sends a shooting ninja star slicing all the way down my side. I leak out a groan that sounds like something that could only come out of a body raised from the dead. Gazes from people in the lobby dart my way. I've never wished to stumble across a sinkhole more than I do in this moment. Except at this point, I don't think I could even stand to fall into one.

"Here's the deal." He stands, squaring his gaze with mine. "You think you can handle it now, but it will get worse when the adrenaline wears off. Unless you get some painkillers, there is no way you'll be able to sleep. Trust me." He holds out his hand, offering me a lift. "It's best to go now while your body is still flooded with adrenaline. If it hurts this bad now, you'll be crawling on the floor in an hour."

I want to rub my eyes, soothing my oncoming headache, but even bending my arm to do that triggers my shoulder to shoot jets of fire down my body. "Maybe."

He quirks a confused eyebrow. "What do you mean, maybe?"

I wag a sassy finger at him as I realize any shred of dignity I'm holding onto is about to go up in flames. "Depends on if I can move."

"Oh, I'll get you there." Without warning, he scoops me off the sofa, the pain so intense even minor movements make my arm shake. I bite down on my lip, resisting the urge to let out another cryptic groan. I hate to admit Noah is right about the pain getting worse as the seconds tick by, but that's the only way I can reason with what's going on in my body. It's like an outer layer of cushion is slowly getting ripped off, leaving the burn of fire from the depths of my core. I'm choking back tears and groans, and my vision starts to go opaque as I lean my head against his chest and allow him to carry me out of the lodge.

I don't remember much about the hospital except for the fact that they gave me the good muscle relaxers as soon as I got to the examination room. One moment I was nearly convulsing from the pain. The next, I was slumped over on the table, leaning on my good elbow, and everything was chill.

I felt completely at ease by the time the doctor popped my shoulder back into place. So much so, I walk out of the clinic with a bubblegum lollipop the nurse gave me. It sticks out of the side of my mouth, and it's definitely the source of my slobber. "I don't know much about medicine," I slur on my way back to Sophie's SUV, "but I think that doctor was a little handsy."

"Nope." Noah's straight face lies. When I squint, I can tell the corners of his eyes crease into a want-to laugh. He's struggling not to laugh at this whole situation. "That was protocol for putting a shoulder back in place."

"Really?" I pause at the passenger door as Noah opens it and places a hand on my forehead for protection—as if I don't know how tall I am.

Five six to be exact.

Or maybe that's metric?

My gaze drops to the floor. Something seems off about that. I look up as I try to see the top of my head. When I find out that's not possible my brows furrow. Noah puts his free hand on my upper arm and guides me forward into the SUV. For no reason other than the fact that I got the good painkillers, I laugh, big and loud.

He leans over me to help buckle me in, and his signature ocean-breeze scent wafts under my nose.

I love the ocean.

The wind.

The sun.

The breeze.

The cute men in swim trunks with deep olive tans. Before I have a chance to filter my words, I word vomit, "I bet you look good in swim trunks."

"Excuse me?" One brow rises higher than the other, and he freezes.

"Oh, I didn't mean it like that. It was a reasonable observation." I flatten my palm to my chest in a humble position. "You were just so fragrant. Like the ocean. Beach. Place. Not like a sewer." I gesture into the silence as I think of a suitable way to explain how random this is, but my brain is fuzzy. It's like they gave me truth serum. The only thing I'm capable of is oversharing all my thoughts that should never be spoken. "You look good anywhere." I smirk as my body is Jell-O, just a glob of mass without bones or even sore muscles.

A shocked chuckle bursts out of him as he shuts the door and runs along to the other side of the car. The drive back to the lodge to meet up with Sophie and Axl is a bit of a haze. These meds make my thoughts so fuzzy and disjointed, I hardly even know what I'm saying. I'm quite sure I didn't shut up for a single second. I blubbered all the way back to the ski resort. I don't even think I muster full sentences. It's more like random words. Nachos. Snuggles. Hot chocolate. Hockey. Kissing. Kissing. Kissing.

After picking up Sophie and Axl, we arrive at our cabin a few minutes later. Noah slips his arm around my waist and gently pulls me from the car.

I'm not a fan of walking.

But I love being in his arms.

Been craving that most of the day, and it's fantastic. Aside from the fact that my feet drag like wet rags made of bricks over the light dusting of snow, Noah does a decent job of tugging me forward. "How many pills did they give you?" he asks.

"Two," I answer. I stare off into space, holding up two index fingers trying to count. "There was one white one and two blue ones."

"That's three." Sophie corrects me as she holds the cabin front door open wide for us, and I pass over the threshold with Noah.

"I think we can agree she had more than enough for all of us," Axl quips as he hangs back, waiting for us to get through the door.

His hands are filled with all our bags, since he was the only one not preoccupied with getting me into the cabin.

Sophie comes up on the other side of me, helping Noah guide me to the couch in the center of the room. She speaks in a soft voice, "I think she needs to rest until some of these meds wear off."

"I'm not tired." I zigzag a medicated index finger at her, and I giggle when I realize it no longer hurts to do that. I do it again because I can.

Sophie gestures for me to walk forward, coaxing me like a toddler who just figured out how to walk. "Just lay down and take a little rest. When you wake up, we'll have some food ready."

Her tone is so soothing that, despite the fact I'm wide awake, I slide my feet toward her. "I feel fine." I plop down on the couch, stretching out. Before I can utter another word, Noah has a flannel blanket swaddled around me. As he tucks it tight around my stomach, I grab his hand and let out a series of giggles, squealing, "That tickles."

"Close your eyes." He sounds hot when he says that, so I listen. Not before I pat the top of his head twice, like he's some domesticated animal. His hair is soft, and it brings more ocean waves . . .

Now that my eyes are closed, I visualize his floating head. He's handsome with his dreamy dark eyes and his plump pouty lips that look so kissable.

Of course, I observe how soft they look.

Wait a second . . .

Am I sleeping or am I talking?

Oh, and did he say if I upgrade the ski plan, we can kiss? I vaguely remember something about that option. The details are fairly opaque.

My thoughts garble together in wave-like patterns.

Or maybe I'm speaking out loud?

Who knows.

Kissing might be nice.

"I need to upgrade to the kissing plan," I say, the words oozing from my mouth as I drift into my dreams.

Nine

NOAH

To allow Paisley privacy to rest, we tiptoe outside to the patio, where there are two padded lawn sofas with a gas firepit in the middle. It's wonderful to have time to sit and do nothing as we joke around, and I lose track of time. We are finishing a pizza when Paisley pads outside in her socks, her flannel blanket wrapped around her like a taco.

Sophie spots her first, her forehead creasing as if she's astonished to see her walking upright. "How are you feeling?"

"Like a zombie. I don't even remember coming here." Paisley blinks, and motions to the pizza. "Any chance I can grab a slice?"

"Go ahead and help yourself. That might help you feel more coherent." Sophie nods to the side table that's stacked with pizza delivery. "Axl ordered, so everything has lots of meat and nothing green."

Using her good arm, Paisley slowly peels out a slice from the first box and takes a bite while standing. She's sure never shy about eating.

"I almost think you had a reaction to your meds." Axl's expression is neutral. "There is no reason you should have been that out of it, unless they gave you the wrong dosage."

"You could be a lightweight," Sophie adds. "That's how I am. I never need more than one baby Aspirin."

"Yep, you are a cheap date." Axl's lips turn up as he teases her.

She ignores him and motions to the empty seat on the sofa next to me. "Take a seat," she tells Paisley.

I'm unusually quiet as I watch her. It's clear by the way she wobbles forward that she's still feeling the effects of her medicine, but it doesn't seem to be as bad as before. At least she's no longer slurring her words. It's hard to forget about the random stuff she blurted out. Like, she talked about kissing the whole drive home. I doubt she remembers saying that, but it left a few ideas in my head. Now I have an even deeper awareness of her nearness. As soon as she plops down next to me, I have to bounce my leg.

Sophie leans casually to engage Paisley. "How is your article going?"

Paisley's lashes lower like she forgot she is awake before springing wide. "I got it done under the deadline right before we left this morning, and that's about all I care about."

"How does that work with your internship?" Axl chimes in. "Are you leaving Mapleton or did Tight ol' Bill offer you a job?"

Paisley shakes her head. "I would love a full-time job offer, but nothing yet."

"Well, if you don't get a job offer, it's nothing against you." Her soft scent pulls me closer, and I place my arm on the back of the sofa. "Bill has this thing where he won't hire interns. He likes people to have more experience."

"Nah," Axl mouths off. "He's cheap and wants another free intern."

"With some things, but you have to remember that she isn't Bill's intern in the first place." I nod, not the least offended for Bill, because it's absolutely true. Even though Bill is rich, he's always been aware of every penny he spends, which is part of the reason he's rich. Not to mention that Paisley was never his employee in the first place, so he won't feel any sense of loyalty to keep her around.

"You can't deny we have the lowest salaries in the AHL." Axl's already finished his pizza, and he's leaning forward, warming his hands near the fire. It's hypnotic to watch the flame swirl around, as it cackles and sparks.

"We are also in last place, so there's that." Most of the time I agree with the guys, but as far as salaries go, it's a math problem. Ticket sales bring in income, and while we keep losing, people aren't buying. "Here's the thing." I never planned on being Bill's cheerleader, but having lived with him for the last year, I have seen a side to him the rest of the guys miss out on. I focus on Paisley as I do my best to clarify again why she likely won't be getting a job offer. "It's a long story, but Bill never wanted to own a hockey team. He wanted to play, and he had the talent and the chance to play in the NHL. He only made it a year before he blew out his back. That should have been the end of it, but he blames his injury solely on one person—Blake Anton—an ex-teammate who he swears sabotaged him. They always had a rivalry."

Paisley jerks back, her eyes spring open, and I pause as she appears to wobble in her seat. "Are you okay?" I place my hand on her shoulder, rationalizing that it's just the meds.

"Ah, yeah. I'm totally fine." Her eyes grow wider yet, but she is silent.

I continue, "It's been years of back and forth, as they faced off for many board positions and even real estate. He'll never admit it out loud, but I suspect Granite Ice was one of the schemes he cooked up to get ahead of Blake. Starting an AHL team might have been going too far because he didn't do it properly to raise capital. It's been a huge drain on his bank account, but you have to hand it to him because he doesn't give up. None of the rivalry makes sense to me. Yeah, he's annoying at times, but aside from being my boss, he's also my stepdad and he's been really good to my mom and me."

Paisley's jaw drops so low it looks as if it lost a hinge.

Sophie and Axl both stare at me, as this isn't the first time they got a mouthful from me about Bill. After a long beat of silence that Paisley makes no attempt to break, Sophie speaks up. "It doesn't matter. You get to play hockey."

The conversation breaks into side conversations when Sophie tells Paisley about her new shoes. Eventually Axl and Sophie disappear inside and off to bed, leaving Paisley, who is fully rested from her nap, and me alone.

"How are you feeling?" I reposition myself again, as I can't seem to get comfortable with her so close to me. It's like my body knows she's there, sparking this magnetic pulse. I want to reach out and hold her, but that's clearly skipping a step.

"A lot better now that I ate. I was so hungry I hardly tasted it." She's wide-eyed, in the middle of a weird stony stare. It piques my nerves a little, as I can tell something is off. The unsettling light in her eyes avoids my gaze.

I sip on my cocoa and let out a slow sigh. "Sorry that I coerced you into coming. I guess I never even asked if you liked skiing."

"Don't apologize." Her tone is serious and dark, void of sarcasm and even the newer flirty inflections I expect from her, but what she says next brings me mixed vibes. "I wanted to hang out with you."

She levels her gaze with mine, and it yields so much force I didn't doubt it could power the entire city of Mapleton. She sways a little toward me. I'm not a doctor but I suspect that has nothing to do with her injury or her medication.

I scoot a bit closer to her. "I'm glad you came, but I'm feeling guilty about putting so much pressure on you to ski. I hope you know you can be honest with me." I scratch the back of my head, when her expression grows distant again. She seems to be in and out of concentration. "Is there something wrong?"

Her lashes waver again, before her gaze drops. Something is up with her. I risk a dumb joke to make her laugh. "Hey, is the sky still up there?"

Her gaze whips back to me, and her eyes narrow into a confused wince. "What?"

"Is the sky up there?"

"It hasn't fallen yet, if that's what you are implying." She leaks out a sarcastic snort, her gaze finds mine, and it's a bit of a lazy look. "You're unreal."

"It made you laugh." I give her my mischievous grin, proud I lifted the mood.

She sputters out another chuckle. I pause to stare into Paisley's fiery eyes as they glint smoky hues of blue. There's nowhere else I'd rather be, and it blows my mind how one person can change your life so fast.

I lean a little bit closer, and she doesn't pull back. Her warmth kindles all around me. She's near-kissing close, and just the simple thought of kissing sends my anxiety to full throttle as I struggle to move. Instead of continuing the conversation, we freeze together.

Her muted sweet scent wafts under my nose, igniting a rumble in my chest. There's only one thing I want to do. My gaze shifts from her eyes to her lips. When she still doesn't move, I consider that an invitation, leaning closer until I seal my lips to hers.

My heart releases a constriction.

After hearing her talk about kissing all afternoon, it's the biggest relief to kiss her.

She quickly slaps her palms on my chest and pushes away from me, her brow lowering into a stare a parent would give a child who was caught red-handed with stolen cookies. Her breathless words rush out, "My father is Blake Anton."

Blinking, my head jolts back. My lips are firing all the tingles, and I struggle to feel my face. It's all gone numb. She wrecked our amazing moment with her horrid timing for admissions.

Blake Anton.

Thud.

She couldn't have said anything more terrifying than that.

I blink, and my memories race. Never once do I remember hearing her last name. How did I miss that?

Sweat slathers my lower back, and I let out a giant sigh of distress.

If there was one thing Bill taught me—and he taught me a lot—he insists that Blake Anton is evil. There's no way Bill or Blake will ever accept any situationship between Paisley and me.

"Talk about an ill-timed confession." I run my fingertips over my lips, glad they are still there. I can't feel them, and I murmur, "Why would you blurt that out now?"

"I knew Bill was your boss, but I had no idea you were related to him." Her breathless heap of words tumbles out. "I couldn't stop thinking about it ever since you mentioned it."

I'm still holding her, and every drop of blood coursing through my veins is screaming this is so much more complicated than I could have ever thought.

My entire job exists solely because Bill wants to get revenge on her dad. There's a collective moment of sobriety where we both seem to hold our breath, and it lasts for several long, agonizing minutes before I do something I would have never seen coming. I finally draw the mental boundary I've been waiting to make for so many years.

This is where I finally make decisions for myself.

I announce as if I'm proclaiming an oath. "Paisley, I don't care about your dad, or Bill. I honestly don't care about anyone but you."

As if to seal my convictions, I lower my lips to press a kiss on her lips. It's impossible not to kiss her when she's in my arms.

As I pull away, a visible swallow clears her throat, and she looks back at me with pining fire in her eyes. Her lips are pinched before her words fall out. "I'm sorry that it never came up. Are you mad?"

The thing is . . . Blake is Bill's enemy. Not mine. I've never actually met the guy. Bill can be awfully dramatic about things.

I shift my hand to her chin, tipping it up. My heart skips a beat that she allows me to do that. What is happening between us feels right. To worry about anything else—especially since all that drama is not even about us—is a waste of my energy. "I'm not mad," I assert. "Maybe a little shocked, but I'm not letting Bill or Anton ruin our weekend." As I rest my chin on her head, soaking up the warmth that wafts off her body, I can't help but let my mind wander.

I mean, Bill isn't going to be happy, and he has a way of getting what he wants, but nothing REALLY bad can happen . . . right?

I've always been an early riser, but I don't think I slept at all, my mind too excited as I replayed our kiss—over and over. My foot bounces under my blanket, reminding me I've now missed two doses of meds. I ignore it, choosing to instead think about our kiss some more.

Maybe I got the timing wrong?

But I don't regret it.

It seemed like we were dangerously close to locking each other into the friend zone if something didn't happen soon. I know she felt the magnetism I did. After stressing about it for another solid ten minutes, I know I'll never settle down. I get up and head to the kitchen, hoping to find some coffee I can make.

Two steps into the living room, and I startle to see Paisley propped up on the living room recliner, fully asleep. Her head leans to one side, supported by a thin pillow folded in half. One foot is on the recliner footrest. The other leg is kicked over the armrest, dangling down. The faintest little snoring pipes out of her nose. It's all too evident she had a rough night.

My heart wrenches with empathy.

More than likely she couldn't sleep flat on her back with her injured shoulder.

Not wanting to wake her, my plans to make coffee are thwarted as the kitchen is just a few steps away from her. But more than that,

I can't help but stare at her. My lips tingle when I recall how it felt to kiss her. She looks so beautiful; I can't help but reach out to brush the side of her cheek. Her skin is so soft, it begs to be kissed, and I lower my face—

And cue her exorcism mode!

Without warning, her head springs back and she jolts to a sitting-up position, pillow already in her hands as she's ready for an attack. Her arm flails back in a windup before her eyes are even open! If the footrest wasn't in her way, I don't doubt she'd be fully standing, her reactions are that quick.

My hands fly up, ready to dodge her weapon. "It's just me," I whisper shout and duck, chuckles ripping out of my mouth. I quickly pinch my lips together because it's not funny she got so scared.

But it actually really is super funny.

Her eyes pop open and swell to the size of silver dollars, all the while she holds this on-guard stance.

A snort leaks as I cover my head and cower. "Relax," I urge in a hushed voice.

"Ah, maybe I should have warned you." Her eyes rapid-fire blink as she quickly scans the room before she brings her gaze back to me. "If you ever want your own episode of Dateline, touch me while I'm sleeping."

I hold my hands up, and all the while I can't stop laughing. After a moment, her shoulders relax, and she slips out a snicker. "What were you trying to do besides get beheaded?"

A deep laugh rolls out of my gut. "I was just brushing my hand against your cheek." My cheeks heat, as it sounds so odd to say that out loud, and I rush to add, "Don't worry. I won't be doing that again anytime soon."

"I would advise not to." She punctuates her words with a curt nod but then rolls her neck into a stretch, as her hand instinctively finds her shoulder and rubs it.

"Rough night?" My gaze hangs on her shoulder. She doesn't look off-kilter anymore, but I can imagine all the bruises and possible swelling she's suffering from.

"Aw man." She tips her head further into a neck stretch, while her jaw drops into a deep yawn. "I have no idea what they gave me at the clinic, but as that wore off, the pain got so much worse. I took some of the pills they sent me home with. Those didn't do near the trick. I couldn't get comfortable." She motions to the chair with a flick of a wrist. "I ended up here, only after trying the couch and even the floor."

"I'm not an expert, but I can tell if it slipped back out of place. I can check if you want."

"I don't think it's out of place." She tilts her head the other way, stretching it more. "But it's not *normal*."

Now that she's dropped her weapon, I advance closer, circling around behind her chair. I slide my hands onto her shoulders, running my thumb along her shoulder blade. It only takes me a moment to feel a dense knot. "I think your shoulder is fine, but you have this knot—maybe it's from how you slept? It could still be from your injury, but I think that's what's bothering you."

Checking my assessment, I press on it, and instantly, she arches her back and pipes out, "Ouch."

"Yep." I chuckle as I wait for her to relax. "That would be it. I can rub it out for you if you want?"

"I'm not going to say *no*." She pulls her hair over her shoulder and turns in her chair to give me a better angle. I get to work, rubbing little circles with my thumb over the knot. "So, I'm guessing it's the hockey that made you an expert on all of this stuff." Her face is angled down, muffling her voice a little, but I can still hear her well enough.

"Many visits to physical therapists over the years. They teach you little tricks to strengthen and stretch your muscles."

Her muscle smooths fast, indicating it is not an old knot, which only further affirms my diagnosis that it's from how she slept.

"Happy Valentine's Day," she says, and a hint of amusement braids into her tone. I can't help but smirk. Even though we aren't officially a couple, it feels just right sitting here with her. "Sorry, I didn't get you a present, but I honestly didn't think we'd be . . . you know."

"It's okay." I speak over her shoulder. "Then I can't get in trouble because I didn't get you anything either."

"I can make breakfast," she quips. "Like, I know how to make some pretty amazing pancakes."

I've never had that feeling that something so simple could be so perfect, but everything about the gesture hits me in the heart. "Breakfast would be the perfect present." I drop my hands from her shoulder and wait for her to stand. As soon as she's to her feet,

I place my hand on her hip. "But first, how about a proper good morning, Valentine's Day kiss."

"A Valentine's Day kiss?" She gives me her mischievous grin and easily slips right into my arms. "Is there anything different about a morning, Valentine's Day kiss?"

"It's just a rule," I tease, hoping she falls for it. She tips her head back and rises to the tips of her toes. Even though adrenaline rapidly fires through my veins, fueling my heart to drum against my chest wall, it honestly feels like the most natural expression for me to pull her in close to me, and seal my lips to hers. Our lips blend together perfectly, and her hand slides up around the back of my neck, leaving a trail of goosebumps over the skin she touched.

I could seriously do this all day.

It's a perfectly valid option.

Since it's Valentine's Day and all.

I mean, I might need a water break after a couple of hours, but I'm pretty sure this is why Valentine's Day was invented—

Jolting away from me, her hand flies to her neck, and her lips bend into a wince. "Sorry," she hisses. "Serious shoulder cramp." Her shoulders bounce on the word cramp as she lets out a defeated chuckle.

"I think I need to rub it more." I match her earlier mischievous grin.

"We don't have anything else to do today." She tips her head to the side, tacking on, "Well, except drive home, but there's no rush." A conspiratorial gleam sparkles out of the corner of her eye. "But let me make breakfast first."

I will never be a guy who turns down food, and I quickly nod. Almost on cue, Axl and Sophie emerge from the hall, and Axl chimes in, "Did someone say breakfast?"

"I did," Paisley replies. "I offered to make pancakes."

"Oh, I'll help." Sophie pivots toward the kitchen. "We have to make them into hearts." She tosses a look back at Axl. "You'll eat pancakes, won't you?"

"As long as they aren't skibiddi."

"Stop." Her hands fly over her ears, but everyone laughs as she mumbles under her breath, "You are no longer allowed to hang out with my brother. He is brainwashing you."

"That's cap." He upnods, with a teasing grin on his face.

Sophie shakes her head while the smile she wears is stretched wide across her face. "Just for that, I'm making you Ohio pancakes," she teases back, and everyone cracks up.

Paisley flashes me the sweetest smile, and it does everything to refuel my own smile. It's like my smile is dependent on hers. I can't help but feel that's the way it's supposed to be. It's not lost on me that I haven't had any anxiety meds for two days, but I've never felt more secure in my decision to allow her to slide into my heart.

After all, that's what this day is for.

Ten

Paisley

It's Monday, the day after we returned from skiing. Not only is it the last day of my assignment here in Mapleton, but it's also the day my magazine spread goes live. I only showed up to my little corner office to clean and turn in my key.

Okay, and to see Noah.

My bags are packed, and I'm about to head back to New York. My heart is squeezed so tightly for so many reasons—the biggest one being Noah.

I knew better than to catch feelings for someone while I was here. Long distance situationships are impossible. Add in the fact that he's a high-profile athlete and travels all the time. I refuse to even think about the family conflict because whenever I try, the breath wrings out of my chest. How did I miss the family relation with Noah and Bill?

Sure, they have different last names, but I should have paid closer attention. I rub my eyes, squeezing down the pressure that's been building. The stress is almost unbearable. I should have never gone on that ski trip. I had no business blending the lines of personal and professional. Shaking my head, my heart thuds against my chest wall as if it's mad for allowing myself to be vulnerable. No matter how hard I tried to fight it, everything about spending time with Noah felt so perfect and even magical. Now that it's over, I know it can't possibly be more than just a weekend thing to him.

I'm counting down the hours until I leave Mapleton, and I can already feel tiny cracks splitting as I prepare to be heartbroken. With a wobbly-knee plop to my desk chair, I click on the Sports Era website. I hold my breath as I wait for it to load. My article is on the top of the first page.

I made the feature article.

I place a shaky hand over my mouth and scroll over the article, soaking in every last ounce of it. It's not the story I had originally wanted to tell. It's not even close to a hit piece. It's all the photos the team's families forwarded to me, and it's about the team excelling.

It's Axl scoring goals, and the guys giving knuckies. It's Jackson's huge smile when he finally blocks a goal. It's Noah—my heart literally pains—skating faster than everyone. It's the families and fans cheering on their feet.

It's exactly what my editor and the team were expecting.

I drop my hand to my keyboard and scroll back. I'm so immensely grateful it's not a hit piece. Flashing my gaze to the heavens, I can't help but smile. Someone was looking out for me when I lost that flash drive. I can't imagine the shame I'd be feeling today if these photos were different . . .

I learned something this last weekend.

Aside from how soft Noah's lips are.

I don't have it in my heart to write a hit piece. As much as I want my dad to "see" me, that's not the way to go about it, and this team is actually a great crew of guys. They may work for Bill Baker, but that's not their fault. They are following their dreams.

A text lights up on my phone. It's my editor.

Steve: You did a great job, Paisley. It was a pleasure to work with you.

I don't even hold back my grin as I text back.

Me: Thank you. It was an honor to work with you.

Steve: Best wishes in your next adventure.

I wait for another text, but when my phone goes dark, I drop my phone to my desk in astonishment.

That's it?

No job offer?

Steve didn't utter a word about applying for something permanent, nor did he offer me a reference. I haven't seen Bill Baker, or anyone else who could offer me a position, and the building is empty.

All that is left is the deafening silence of my time in Mapleton being over.

I swallow, about to find myself in self-pity again, but my attention turns to the doorway. Noah strides straight toward me with the full smile on his face I've learned to love. He soundlessly steps forward, as if he's walking on air, and doesn't stop until he's in my personal space bubble. His eyes glint a dark hue of aged copper, and my vision decides now is the perfect time to morph into a milky haze.

This weekend was a dream, which I can't believe I haven't woken up from. I half wince as I stand. I'm so scared he's going to blow me off, but he wraps an arm around my waist, pulling me into an embrace, and drops a chaste kiss to my lips.

My heart trips and I'm so incredibly grateful he's still here. When he pushes a magazine toward me, I ask, "What's this?"

"It's my issue." He pushes it farther at me and hands me a pen. "I had to go to three gas stations this morning to find a hard copy, but I got one, and I want you to sign it."

My heart swells, pumping full of so many tiny hearts. It's not the glowing recognition I had dreamed of from my dad, but this is better. I roll my bottom lip in and take the magazine from his hands. I don't need to check the page numbers as I know I'm on the first page, and I instinctively flip to my spread and sign it with my loopy cursive.

The girl you won't meet twice.

As I pass it back to him, the smirk he gives me almost melts me to the ground. He sort of wobbles left and right, reaching his arm out, before saying, "I'm running late for practice but I wanted to catch you before you leave. Is there any way you can make it to the charity banquet tonight? The social is at six, and if you need to leave early, I understand."

"Is Bill going to be there?" My teeth slide over my lip, digging in with force.

After a curt nod, his expression turns stony, and he rasps, "I'm not going to hide this, and I'm not making apologies to anyone. He might as well get used to it now."

"Does he know?" I slowly tip my head toward him, my eyes growing wider. I start to go off about how bad this is going to be for him, but my words get stuck because I'm still in his arms. I can't worry about anything when I'm here. I wrap my arms around his neck and let him decide.

"I don't care. I don't have to quantify anything to anyone." He shrugs, as his fingers find my cheek. "He should know. Everyone should know."

I can't say I love Noah, because it's a little early for that, but I adore him. Hearing him proclaim all that without even so much as a hesitation, I am done.

Gone.

My gaze falls to his lips, and I allow myself a moment to pause and let the newness sink in as anticipation fires in my chest. I deserve that fleeting pause before I rise to my toes and press my lips to his.

I can tell by the urgency in his lips that Noah isn't going anywhere. If Noah can stand up to Bill Baker, I can certainly handle my dad.

I hope.

Taking a final lap around the arena as a way of saying goodbye, I walk slowly, a heaviness settling on my chest by the time I make it to the parking lot. I didn't do anything close to what I set out to do, but somehow, I'm prouder. However, that pride doesn't conceal the niggling in my gut that pings harder when my phone rings and I see my dad's name.

I could silence it and let it go to voicemail.

That might make him worry, and I would hate for him to panic and reach out to someone at the magazine and cause a scene. Remorsefully, I accept the call and tuck the phone between my ear and shoulder as I continue to stride across the parking lot. "Hey, Dad."

"You're all done, huh?" His voice is boisterous, void of the upset I was suspecting.

"Officially, yes." I dig into my pocket, pull out my car keys, and take a moment to unlock my door before I get in. It's way too cold to stand outside to chitchat. "I accepted an invitation to their banquet tonight. That will get over sort of late, so I'll check out of my Airbnb tomorrow, and head home."

"That's nice the team invited you."

I can't tell by his tone if he's fishing, but I also know there's no point in delaying conversations that need to be had. I'm not embarrassed by Noah, and the more I ponder this, I think it's better to break the news slowly . . . and over the phone. That will give him the chance to get used to the idea. "It wasn't the team who invited me; it was just one guy. He's invited me to be his date—Noah." I shut my lips tight, as that might be enough of a hint for now. He doesn't need to know Noah is related to Bill. I'm not trying to give him a heart attack.

"Is the date part of your undercover sting?" Dad's voice is even, unreactive.

It will be so easy to say yes and be done with this conversation, but that isn't going to help me in the long run. I swallow and offer only, "No. Since my article is published, I'm done with that. This is a date."

"I don't understand." His breath is getting heavy, evident by how I can hear snippets of it through the phone, and I decide that's enough information for now. Easy does it.

"It's okay, Dad." I soften my tone, hoping to slow his heart rate. "It's just a date."

"Well, be careful not to get attached. It doesn't make sense for you to be spending time with anyone when you live in New York. Not to mention, these guys aren't what you see. They may be all charm to you, but they're not anybody you want to get involved with."

First, it's a little too late for that.

Second, you're wrong about Noah.

Third, I didn't ask for your advice.

The words I'm able to speak are at war with my thoughts and I only manage, "I know."

"Well, text me tomorrow when you get on the road."

"I will." My finger is already on my phone, ready to end the call when I add, "Love you. Bye." I can't think about my dad right now. I need to get to the banquet, and dwelling on all the what-if scenarios is only going to stress me out. At least for tonight, I want to enjoy my time with Noah, while he celebrates with his team.

I start my car, and I shift it into gear. I'm about to pull out of my parking space when a small envelope on my windshield catches my eye.

How did I get a parking ticket?

I shift back into park and open my door enough to stick my arm through the crack to retrieve the envelope. The girth of the envelope surprises me, and my brows dip as I study the package. There are no markings of any kind. When I flip it over, the only thing I see is the flap to open it. I slide my finger in, ripping it gently, and pull out a small stack of printed photos.

I see a zoomed-in image of Axl punching a player.

Another image shows Axl with his face so close to a ref, he looks like he's about to headbutt him. The hairs on the back of my neck stand up. I've seen these images before.

I took them.

My fingers shake as I fan through the small stack, and I recognize every single photo. These are my photos. It's everything I lost on my memory card, and every single one of them is taken from an angle that makes the guys and the whole team look terrible.

Nausea rocks my stomach. I drop the photos to my lap and cover my mouth with my hand. Who has seen these?

Does Noah know?

If he does know, how could he possibly not hate me?

Questions pelt me like bees, each one stinging more than the last.

Sliding down in my seat, my brain still in shock, my gaze slides outside my window, and I search the dark shadows.

Is someone watching me?

A lump forms in my throat and my body stiffens. I slide my finger to my door lock and click on it. No longer feeling safe, I jerk my car into gear and speed out of the parking lot, my mind running with so much fear.

Headlights flash on behind me, and a car pulls out. Maybe it's a coincidence, or maybe my mind is running wild. Whether they are following me or not, someone has my memory card. That someone knows what I was up to. They apparently don't want to be quiet about it anymore.

But why?

Eleven

Noah

Paisley: I'm running late. Still coming.

I reread her text and lower my phone to the table, loosening my tie to allow in more air. It's banquet night, and the entire team and their families are stuffed in a hotel conference room with long tables that are squished together with zero air flow. I reach for my water glass, and I bounce my leg up and down underneath the table.

Paisley is still not here, but guess who is?

The woman Bill invited for me.

Yep, forgot about her.

Katie or Kinsley . . . I can't even remember her name. She's smiling at me from across the table, and every few minutes she bats her lashes and tries to make small talk. It's not her fault she got swept into Bill's plan.

This is what he does.

"I watched all your home games this season." Once again, she leans forward, flashing me a big-teeth smile. Even if Paisley wasn't on her way here, I don't want to flirt with this person.

"Hmm?" I grunt out, barely looking in her direction. What am I supposed to say? That this is a mistake? She needs to go home. Sweat beads on my brow as I scan the room for Paisley again.

We finish listening to Coach Carlson give his welcome speech. It wasn't his worst one, but it also wasn't anything I haven't heard before. Coach takes his seat, and now it's Bill's turn to ramble. Bill's the only guy in the room not wearing a tie as he opted for a Granite Ice Polo shirt and trousers. I guess you can set your own dress code when you own the team.

"Good evening, everyone." Bill nods a few times from his place at the podium.

As I stare at him, I can't help but feel a tinge of resentment. I've never felt this way about him before, but it almost seems like I'm thinking clearer now than I ever have. Maybe it's because I'm off my meds, but who knows.

Karen, or whatever her name is, flicks her hair over her shoulder, trying to get my attention. I wonder if Bill paid her to sit by me and act like that? It's not above his character if there's something in it for him, especially since he's done it before. Needing to sulk, I slide my elbow onto the table and drop my chin into my palm. I think it's time to move.

Move to a different table where it's not so crowded.

And I need to move out of Bill's house.

And if it was up to me, I would move to another team.

The crazy thing is that I almost got signed into the NHL, but I was so worried about leaving my mom that when the scouts came, my anxiety went through the roof. I couldn't handle the pressure, and I purposely blew a few too many passes. As I slouch down in my chair and survey the room, I feel my mistake deep in my gut. This team is going nowhere. If I stay for another year, I'll be stuck and nobody will ever take me seriously.

My gaze hitches on a black shape outside the ballroom doors. At a second glance, I confirm it's Paisley. She always wears black, and her long hair hangs down, fanning all around her. I flash a silent two-finger wave and scoot my chair back. There is no way I'm going to have her come over here and get the wrong idea about Kayla or Kitten or whatever her name is. Speaking of what's-her-face, she stares at me with wide eyes, and I freeze before I mumble, "Ah, sorry, I'm not feeling the best."

Before she has a chance to pull me back, I race out of the room. I'm out the door, scanning in all directions. She was here a second ago. I spin on my heel and almost run smack into her. "Hey!" I call out and quickly relax as I lean in for a hug and drop a kiss on her cheek. I'll never tire of doing that. "Glad you made it."

"Sorry, I'm late." Her lashes flutter as she struggles to meet my gaze, and it's all over her pale face that something isn't right.

I drop my hand to her hip. "What's going on?"

Her lips pinch together and her gaze angles away, and for the slightest of moments, I think she's mad about Kasey. Kacy. Whatever her name is, and I blurt out, "That lady I was sitting with is someone Bill invited. I don't even know her name."

She glances behind me as if searching for someone. "I didn't notice anything." Her face doesn't even bend toward the room as she finally directs her gaze at me, and whispers, "Maybe I'm overreacting, but I think I have a stalker."

My brows pull up, as that's the last thing I expect to hear. "Why do you think so?"

"Do you remember when I lost my camera, and then when I got it returned, the memory card was missing?"

My ears hyper-attune as alarms go in my head. "Yes."

"When I got in my car earlier, there was a small packet on the windshield. At first, I thought it was a parking ticket, but it was my photos." She holds up her index finger. "Not the memory card like they wanted to return it to me. Instead, just a few of them printed out and no note."

"Well, that's a good thing if someone found your photos, right?" I gesture forward. "I mean, you already turned in your article, but it's nice to have them back."

"Look." She inhales a deep breath, and her shoulders fall on her exhale. When she looks back at me, her fiery eyes are potent. "I'll be honest. I had a variety of photos on that camera, and the prints they left on my car were some of the worst ones. Ones I'd never want anyone to see. It feels like blackmail."

That's sketch.

My mind rolls through all the possible images she can have, but it seems silly, and I'm confused. "What do you mean 'blackmail'?"

"Nothing really bad, like inappropriate photos." Her cheeks flame red. "I took photos through all the games. Since you guys lost a lot, most of the photos weren't painting you guys in the best light. So, it almost feels like they are trying to . . . I don't even know the right word, but it doesn't feel helpful. Why not just give me my memory card? Plus, when I was leaving, I swore a car followed me, and now I'm scared to be alone."

Anger bubbles in my gut as it doesn't sound like a coincidence. At some point she must have made an enemy. Nobody would do this unless they were trying to mess with her. "Do you know anyone in Mapleton that you upset?"

"Not really, but it would need to have been someone at the gala, or there shortly after, to get my camera." She stares off in the distance as she jabs the end of her thumbnail between her teeth.

I don't usually get alarmed by much, but a spiral of goosebumps snakes up my spine, irritating my nerves. I don't want her to go anywhere alone. I actually don't want her here at all, and I blurt out, "I know you have to get back to New York, but I don't want you leaving tonight. Someone might be following you."

Her eyes swell even rounder. "I wasn't going to leave until morning, because it's a five-hour drive."

"I think you should stay at my house." Someone might be listening to us. I scan the hall, finding it still empty, but I drop my voice anyway. "If they know where you work, you can bet they know where you've been staying."

She stares past me, as if studying something down the hall. "Maybe just for this one night. Just to be safe."

I take her hand in mine and slide a foot toward the door. "Let's get out of here."

While jerking her thumb back over her shoulder, a look of remorse flashes on her face. "What about the banquet?"

"It's fine." I don't look back. "I'm not missing anything. It's just a bunch of people in expensive clothes." I don't tell her that my gut is uneasy for her, and that it's crawling up my throat.

I'm an absolute idiot for not refilling my meds.

Why was I thinking that I would be fine?

I've been busy, but it's not an excuse.

I swallow, forcing all my anxiety down, yet again. All I want to do is get her somewhere safe, where I know we aren't being watched. Maybe I've watched too many thriller movies, but everything about this screams stalker.

I usher her out the door, mapping a route to my house that's different than my usual one in case anyone is following us. All these horrid thoughts jumble in my head, and my heart putters fast, sounding alarms.

With the exception of the security lights above the garage and the single light shining out from under the front door, my house is dark when I pull into the garage. "Home sweet home."

Paisley's unnatural pale hand finds her door handle, and she gets out. My heart drums against my chest, and my gaze scans all around the massive eight-stall garage, as I search for anything out of the ordinary. "Ah, this way." I gesture toward the door while I wait for her, and then wrap an arm around her waist as soon as she meets up with me.

I open the door slowly, pushing my nose first, and sigh when I see Puck lying in his spot. It's a secure feeling, even though Puck is old. Nothing will ever get past him. I sigh as I bend to pat his head. "This is Puck, Bill's dog."

"Wait a second." Her gaze skirts side to side. "This is Bill's house?"

I nearly choke. I forgot to clue her into that part. How she could think this mansion is mine makes me almost snort. "I'm staying here this year to save money. It was either that or get a second job. I didn't want to be exhausted from working all the time and have it affecting my game."

"Ah, okay." Her feet slide together into a proper stance.

"You can relax." I raise my hand, inviting her further into the house. "He's not even home. He's at the banquet, and I'm sure they will be out for a while." My heart is beating so hard that I place my hand against it and pray it doesn't explode. When I got out of bed this morning, I didn't plan on having to run off a stalker.

Paisley's eyes lock on my hand over my heart, and her lips part, but she's silent.

I scan along the floor for an inkling of a clue to where Puck put my meds. I can't believe I overlooked this all day today, and it's all coming to catch up with me now. I walk around the perimeter of the adjacent living room, close the curtains on the huge bay window, and double check all the locks on the windows. Then I pace back to the kitchen and suck back a deep breath, which does nothing to loosen what feels like a vice grip on my lungs. "Let's, ah, sit down." I nod back toward the sofa in the living room. "Can I get you a water or anything?"

It's not even the thought of the stalker that is making me this paranoid, but my anxiety is ramping up with each second. The more I try to slow my breath, the more it ticks up.

"Nah, I'm good for now." She pads forward soundlessly, while I steady myself with one hand on the counter and open the fridge door with the other to grab a chilled bottle of water. I open it and down about half of it in one pull, but my chest cinches tight. When I join her on the sofa, I plop down, a full sweat on my brow. My ears are hyper-attuned to every creak in the floor, and I'm imagining all that could go wrong.

"Are you okay?" Paisley drops her hand to my leg, and I take it in my hand and give it a squeeze.

"I'm a little concerned. Maybe we should call the hotel to see if they know the name of the person who dropped off the camera?" I'm already reaching in my pocket for my phone as I can't believe I haven't thought of this sooner, but it's the perfect solution.

"I already called." Her eyes are wide, bringing a warning.

"And?"

"Ah, they didn't know a thing about the camera. They said it never turned up."

"And you're just telling me this now?" My spine straightens, pinging each vertebra with a little hammer to prick at all my nerves.

I don't even know how it's possible, but my chest cinches even more. "It has to be someone from the maintenance crew or maybe the DJ service. Do you know who cleans that place?"

"I was there for less than an hour. I don't know anything." She shakes her head, and her gaze seems to dance over my face before her voice drops. "I'm sorry to worry you. Maybe I should call my dad? I don't want you to think you have to stress out about this."

The last thing I need is her dad coming over here, and Bill finding him. "Nah, it's fine." I slice my hand through my hair and run it along the back of my neck, but it does nothing to calm me. My mind seems to have a block on it, as I can't focus on anything except for my heart pounding so hard against my chest. "Say." I stand, doing my best to sound calm. "I'm going to run upstairs to look for something."

"Okay." Her expression is neutral, but I feel her gaze follow me out the door. As soon as I'm out of sight, I sprint up the stairs two by two and scurry into the bathroom. I pull out a drawer and dig my hand way to the back, searching for meds. Maybe my mom found them and put them in here.

Nothing.

Sweat dots my forehead, and I open the medicine cabinet. Nothing but over-the-counter cold medicine and lots of mismatched sports wraps.

I grab my chest as I leave the bathroom. The walls seem to wave, and my breathing is hard, but I cross the hallway in a hurry and head toward my mom and Bill's room. It's super cringe to go in here, but it's the only place I haven't looked. With Puck up to his games, I don't doubt he could have stashed them somewhere.

My gaze traces the dressers and the door to the walk-in closet. I hate to snoop in their private stuff, but if I know Puck, he more than likely stuffed it in a corner or behind a nightstand. I'm careful not to touch anything as I peek behind the door, but there's nothing but the usual jam. I pace forward with my gaze set on the four-poster bed, and I drop to the floor and squint, a pile of disorganized stuff coming into focus. I reach my hand under and pull out a beanie.

Palmer City Voltage?

That's totally sus.

Bill would never allow this in his house. He hates the Voltage.

My eyebrow quirks.

Or does he?

I've often suspected his hate was more of a front for jealousy. I reach my hand under again and pull out a Voltage jersey. Now, I crack a smile as this isn't an accident. He clearly has a secret love for them. I push my hand under another time, and my fingers meet something I instantly recognize to be mine.

I almost shout with joy when I pull out my meds and hold them to my chest, as if the proximity to my heart has the power to slow my pounding heartbeat. I'm already standing up when I whip around to get out of here and wham!

I crash into Bill.

"Excuse me." I fumble, holding my pills up. "I've been missing these for days, and I knew Puck hid them." I kick the beanie, doing my best to push it back under the bed without him seeing I found out his secret. "I didn't see anything else."

His gaze angles down in a wide sweep, his nerves evident by his brow pinned together as he checks his side of the bed. Thankfully, it's clear. The air is thick as I slide my feet toward the door, hurrying along.

"We missed you at the banquet." Bill's tone is neutral.

"Ah, sorry. I wasn't feeling well." I hold my pills up again, thankful to have tangible proof to show him. "I haven't had any meds in days. Everything caught up to me."

"I saw Paisley downstairs."

"Yeah, I invited her to hang out."

"I'm about ready to turn in for the night and watch the news." He nods toward his bed, a kind smile on his face. "I hope you feel better."

"Thanks." My fingers tighten around the bottle. This time my feet don't stop until I get to the bathroom. I fill a large cup of water and swallow my pill. Relief washes over me as I know I dodged a panic attack. I turn the faucet on, letting it run for a minute before I lower my face over the sink basin and splash cold water on it.

I'm already feeling better when I emerge from the bathroom to return to Paisley. Hopefully, my mind clears up, and I can figure out how to help her.

Twelve

Paisley

I pace around the circumference of Noah's living room, phone tucked to my ear. "I know what you are saying, Dad. I'm trying not to worry too much."

"I would worry," he responds, his gruff voice ticking up a notch. "There are a lot of weirdos out there. The fact that they held onto the photos for so long tells me they have a plan of some sort. You didn't find any notes or anything? Did you look all around your car in case it blew away?"

"Nothing." Goosebumps dot my spine because that's the thing that bothers me the most. Without a note, I have no idea what this person is trying to accomplish.

"I don't think you should be staying alone anymore. Can you come back here and stay with your mom and me?"

"I don't want to leave until morning because it's dark already, but Noah was concerned too, so he insisted I stay at his place for the night."

Silence, before I hear how that sounds to my old-fashioned dad. "It's not like a bachelor pad. He lives with his mom and . . . stepfather." I purposely retract Bill's name as I cringe, holding back every intention I had of being honest about Noah's relationship to Bill. I'm going to tell him about it, but I wasn't planning on also getting a stalker. Too much stress at one time will kill my dad.

"Noah?" His voice crescendos. "The same guy you went on a date with?"

"Yeah." Folding my lips in, I now regret even telling my dad about the stalker. He had called, and I was still upset, and he could hear something in my voice. When he asked me what was wrong, it slipped out. Now I regret answering the phone.

"Don't you think the timing is a little weird for all of this? You start dating this guy, and now you have a stalker."

"It has nothing to do with Noah." I shake my head vehemently. I know that as fact. If it has to do with anyone, I guess it is my dad since I'm here working for him, and he does have an interesting way of doing business, making many enemies.

"I don't like this one bit, but you're a grown woman." An audible sigh waves through my phone. "Let me know when you get on the road in the morning. I'm glad your travel assignment is over. It's time for you to come home."

"I will." Noah's footfalls coming down the stairs sound in the background, and I push the conversation to end. "I'll text in the morning. Love you." I press end on the call right as I turn to Noah.

He jerks a thumb over his shoulder. "Did you see Bill come in?"

"Briefly." My eyes trace the invisible trail he created when he motioned to the steps. My heart feels heavy being in this house after everything I had planned to do to hurt Bill. "They came in and said hi and reiterated that I am welcome. He said something about a carnival this weekend that I was invited to and then went upstairs."

"Oh, yeah, another one of Bill's charity things. He takes his charity work almost as seriously as hockey." Noah's gaze dances over my face as if he's studying me. "You're welcome to come if you want."

I hang my head as guilt washes over me. When I accepted this assignment to come to Mapleton, I only had one mission—to make my dad proud. I never thought about the people who I would be hurting. I know now with every ounce of blood in my body I would never be able to intentionally hurt anyone. The thing is, before I came here, the team didn't feel like real people. It was like fictional characters made out to be villains, with Bill as their headmaster. I loved to despise them because that's the story I was always told.

I lock eyes with Noah, and shame overcomes me. With those pictures in someone's hands, it might be only a matter of time before they are exposed in a more public way.

This might be my only chance to explain to Noah.

I want to give him an explanation not to cover myself, or make excuses, but to let him know I was wrong and that I had an awakening. And it was largely because of the kindness he showed me.

"It's going to be okay." Noah effortlessly wraps both arms around me. "Mapleton's a really safe town. If anything, it might be some high school punks playing a joke on you. There's no reason anyone would want to hurt you. You're the nicest person."

I swallow, pressing my cheek into Noah's chest, wishing his words were true. Every one of them stabs at my heart, echoing all the bad intentions I had. He's going to find out sometime. If I have any chance of salvaging his trust, it needs to come from me.

It's now or never.

"That's not exactly true." I suck back a deep breath. "There is something I did wrong."

"You did nothing wrong." His smile only increases, and he lowers his face. "This isn't even about you. This is one stupid person being dumb."

My heart thuds against my chest as little quakes of nerves rumble in my belly. It'll be fine. Noah is the nicest guy I know. He'll probably laugh it off. "Here's the thing—" His eyes are so wide and brimmed with trust that it makes me cut myself off. Taking a deep swallow, I try a different approach. One less direct. "Did I tell you the magazine I'm working for is actually owned by my dad?"

His lips roll in, and he shakes his head. "Nah, I don't recall."

"It is." My gaze bounces to the floor before I continue. "My dad and I get along fine and everything, but I have four brothers who all play hockey." I raise my brows in punctuation and tack on, "You know from Bill how obsessed with hockey my dad is, right?"

"Oh yeah."

"I don't know." Even though I'm still in his arms, I stare past him as there is no way I could ever look at him and say this. "I always felt invisible around my dad. When I was little, it didn't bother me, but as I got older, I really started to resent it. I was jealous of the extra love and attention my brothers got." A knot of inferiority swells in my gut, and it hurts to acknowledge all of this out loud—and to Noah, who I only recently got to know, but now I care what he thinks of me.

"Your father is a fool to make you feel like that." The unwavering conviction in his voice only makes my heart constrict more.

"Maybe I am a fool." I can't fathom what I was even thinking a month ago when this assignment was handed to me. "I did something really stupid."

A light chuckle leaks from his lips. "How stupid?"

"This isn't a joke." I practically speak over him, because I'm so ashamed. I can't stand to have him defend me right now. I inhale slowly, knowing there is no way out of this but with the truth. Not if I want a shot of having a genuine relationship with Noah. "I agreed to come to Mapleton to write for my dad's magazine, but I was assigned to write a hit piece," I blurt out, rapidly and jumpy like I'm pulling a trigger to a pistol I'm forced to shoot. "All the photos I had on the memory card are bad photos I took, with the intention to make you all look like jerks."

I squint, as if lowering my eyelids puts a shield over my heart.

His head cocks to the side, as if my words are still ringing in the ear closest to me, but then slowly trickle down through his body until they reach his fingertips, where I can feel his grip around my waist tense up. This sends an immediate beam of fear to rocket back through me. "I would never do it, though! I saw how amazing this team is, and I regret even agreeing to it."

One hand of his drops, as it seems some nervous energy has shot into his body, and he slices his hand through his hair and gives me an angled look.

Still speechless.

"Look," I say, taking a defensive tone. "I only know about Bill from my dad's point of view. You know their rivalry. I was trying so hard to impress my dad, but now I don't care what he thinks, and I would never—" I physically cross my heart with my finger "—ever do anything to intentionally hurt you."

His brows bend down, and he releases his other hand from my hip, pulling his eye contact too. I panic and leak a laugh. Not because it's funny but because I'm desperate to have him say something to me. "It's sort of funny, right?" I nudge him with my elbow, but he's stiff, backing away from me. "It's like I had someone looking out for me when my card got stolen."

Finally, his gaze slams into mine, and his eyes are wide, vulnerable. I'm about to breathe a sigh of relief that he's finally coming to my rescue one more time! He'll save me from my own confession. His lips purse out into a contemplative fold that forewarns what's coming.

My heart feels a prick, small at first, but it grows in intensity until a slow pressure exchange begins, and it starts to deflate. I reach for his hand, grabbing for anything to stop the release, but he pushes my hand away and turns his head. "Noah," I plead with shaky breath. "I'm sorry. I didn't know you."

"I guess I didn't know you either," he whispers, taking a heart-deflating step back.

I trap my bottom lip between my teeth, giving him time to process this. It's a lot to consider, but I don't doubt he'll understand things. He runs his hand through his hair again, and barely tosses a look over his shoulder. "This is Bill's house. I think you need to leave."

"What about my stalker?" I blurt out, still afraid I'm in danger. "I was hoping if I told you the truth about the photos, you'd be able to help me figure this out."

When he pivots to look at me, it's as if his eyes can't even focus. "Maybe call your dad back. He seems to have the answers you like."

"Noah," I whisper shout, not wanting to wake anyone upstairs. "Don't you get it? I don't want to do what he says anymore. That's why I confessed."

He blinks, as if coming out of a trance, and finally focuses on me but only for a moment. Then his feet slide back through the hallway, and he calls over his shoulder, "I'll give you a ride to your car. You should be fine until morning."

He can't be serious.

This is Noah.

He rescued me every single time I didn't need him to. And now, the time I could use his empathy, he's a stone wall. "Noah," I call after him, but he's unwavering in his path to the door. Giving up, I drag my feet after him because he's already halfway through the kitchen.

With my face angled down, I follow him to his car, and we ride in silence until he pulls up behind my car. Not even putting his car into park, he stares straight ahead, waiting for me to get out.

I'm terrified to go back to my Airbnb. I won't get any sleep. Not with my mind reeling like this. My shaky fingers find my door handle, but I toss a look back at him. Apparently, Noah can put up a great stone wall, but I offer a last very quiet, "I know it may seem like I'm only sorry everything had to come out with this stalker, but that's not why I'm sorry at all. I'm sorry I trusted my dad. I knew better."

His Adam's apple moves up, marking his deep swallow. Not wanting to be a bother, I open my door and slip out of his car, resigning to the fact I have a long drive ahead of me.

I failed this assignment.

Not the photojournalism one.

The life lesson one.

My hands tremble as I climb into my car and shift into drive again. I'm actually grateful I ran out of gas earlier this week. Since then, I've been leaving my gas tank topped off, which makes it easy for me to jump directly onto the interstate to return home.

Thirteen

Noah

I take deep noisy inhalations as soon as she slams my car door.

I'm not a jerk.

I'm also not okay with letting Paisley stay by herself tonight, but the bigger truth is I'm not okay myself.

My meds haven't kicked in, and I can't let her see that my anxiety is soaring so much that my body is breaking down. Measured breathing usually is enough to get me back to baseline, but it does nothing. I close my eyes to start my visualization exercises. There's no way I could be this weird in front of her. Light flickers, and my curiosity piques enough for me to open one eye. Her taillights speed out of the parking lot, taking a north turn back toward the interstate.

She can't drive to Long Island tonight.

I shake my head, hating that I can't function. I thought she'd go back to her rental. That's too far to drive, and she still doesn't know if she's safe. I roll my lips in, hoping she at least calls her dad back to let her know she's on her way. She's a grown woman, though, and it's probably best she be near family.

I speed back to my house, making it back in record time. I hurry through the door and step over Puck, who's oddly passed out on his side with his nose buried into the blanket that covers his plush dog bed.

It's back to my bathroom for another dose of my meds. It hadn't dawned on me before that I might need a loading phase for the first couple of days since I had weaned off of them. With a quick flick of my wrist, I snap the light on, and my eyes jolt open wide.

The bottle is not on the counter where I had left it.

Not again.

I shake my head vigorously. The source of my anxiety might very well be living with a kleptomaniac bulldog. I quickly check the medicine cabinet to be sure. When that turns up empty, I don't waste time barreling back down the hall to wake up the culprit.

No wonder he was so tired that he never woke up. With the way he's been wearing me out with all these games, he must be exhausted. I scramble past Bill's closed bedroom door, pausing only in my mind to rule that out. I already searched in there once. I doubt Puck would reuse the same hiding spot.

I make it to the kitchen with my hand on my chest and grumble in a loud voice with every intention of waking up that dog, "Puck, where are my pills?"

His body shivers as he rolls to an upright position and snaps his gaze on me, fake sneezing in annoyance.

"That's right," I growl, advancing toward him, ready to show this fifty-pound mutt who is boss. "I know you have my bottle again, and it's not funny."

Another fake sneeze but this one is laced with anger.

"I'm not letting you sleep." I drop to my hands and knees, getting down on his level, and push my face up to his. In desperation, begging is not out of the question. "You need to show me where you put my pills." I blink, realizing if anyone saw me face off with a dog like this, I would be laughed at.

His large brown eyes lock on me, and I know he understands exactly what I'm saying. "Show me," I urge, sitting back on my heels as I ready myself to follow him. His lips spread wide into that rascal smile he gets when he's loving the attention. He darts down the hall, straight toward Bill's closed office door, stopping in front of it to scratch at it with his paw.

"You think you're so sneaky." My voice is already calmer now that he's cooperating with me. I pad down the hall as quietly as I can and slip my hand onto the doorknob. It's unlocked and the door easily pushes open. I've only ever been here a handful of times, as this is another place that feels off-limits, but I'm desperate and Bill's asleep anyway.

I don't hesitate to do what I need to, and I stand back, allowing Puck to go inside. He waddles to the middle of the room and turns around, eyes hooking on me while his tail wags. I'm so over stalling, and I lower my voice to command, "Show me."

He goes right to the corner, a small space between the black leather couch and the wall. There's enough room for him to wiggle his round body inside, and it instantly makes sense. It's almost funny how he finds these spots that are so perfect for him. If I wasn't so out of breath, I might actually laugh. He crawls back out, his paws leading the way. His jaw is clenched tight with something, and I'm prepared to breathe a giant sigh of relief. But instead, my heart plummets.

It's not what I was expecting him to pull out . . .

It's an envelope, more than likely some junk mail he stole from the trash, and I drop to my knees, resisting the urge to cry. I just can't beg anymore. "Puck, what else do you have?" I push past him and shove my arm into the crack. Sure enough, there's my bottle. My gaze flashes to the heavens. I'm so thankful that I vow to never leave them unlocked again. It's just not worth it.

I scramble to my feet, ready to jet back upstairs to take my pill and salvage any sleep I can get tonight, but Puck stands there and growls at me, the envelope still in his jaw.

"What is it now?" I reach down, not expecting him to give it to me, but he walks right over and drops it at my feet. I don't want Bill to suspect I'm rummaging in his office, so I pick up the envelope with every intention of putting it back, but pictures spill out . . .

Granite Ice hockey photos.

I raise one eyebrow as my eyes shift side to side before they drop back down and browse the photos. Goosebumps dot my spine. When my gaze lands on a random memory card, I solve this riddle.

Well, well, well . . . what do I have here?

My lips roll in, as I can't believe I hadn't suspected him earlier. Of course, Bill would remain silent about what he saw, and he doesn't deal with problems in any normal rational way. It makes so much sense that he'd be passive aggressive about this.

"Good boy, Puck," I say, my tone soothing over the tension we had between us. I pat his head and his little body wiggles all over. "You found Paisley's stalk—"

"What's all the commotion down here?" Bill stands in the open doorway, wearing a long-striped nightshirt that hangs just below his knees, leaving his hairy legs exposed. It's a vision no one should ever have of their boss. I quickly cut my gaze to his face. One of his eyes is sleepily narrower than the other, but they are both firmly planted on me.

Standing up straight up again with the photos still in hand, I present my bottle as evidence. "Puck stole my anxiety pills again. He showed me where he put them, right here in your office." I'm about to slide my foot toward the door and avoid this drama, but everything in me says Bill needs to be called out. I slide my other hand in front of him, flashing the envelope. "Did you lose something?"

Both his eyes spring wide open as his gaze drifts from Puck to me back to his desk. With a stutter on his tongue, he musters, "I-I didn't think I did."

"I found them in the crack between the sofa and the wall. I'm assuming Puck put them there, but how did you get them?"

One of his brows hike into a contemplative angle, tipping me off that he might be making this up, but I listen. "I found it," he asserts with a curt nod.

"Obviously." I throw my hand out in an impatient gesture. "Where was it?"

"At the gala." His head bobs south, in the direction of the hotel. "Look, she's not who you think she is. She's Blake's daughter, and she was here on some spy mission."

"Not a spy mission." I roll my eyes at Bill's dramatics. "It was her job." My gaze dips to the floor for a moment before I continue. "Paisley confessed to me that she tried to write a hit piece, but she changed her mind. How did you know about any of this?"

"It was too odd how she called me and asked to come study the team." He shakes his head, a smirk growing on his face. "I'm not as dumb as you young kids think I am. I'm not going to let just anyone interview my team. I did some background checks on her and quickly uncovered who she was related to."

"You knew who she was this whole time?" Disbelief settles in my gut. "Why did you let her come?"

One of his shoulders raises and lowers in an uncommonly slow shrug. "I figured she'd write the article if I said yes or not. If I welcomed her to work with us, I could at least keep an eye on her. It didn't take me long to see she wasn't interested in showing the team's good side. She refused to take the shots I asked her to take, but she was always right there with that camera in front of her face whenever one of you got in trouble. At the gala, I was watching her, and I saw her fall. Everything happened so fast. When you pulled her out, I noticed her camera was still on the ground, and I grabbed it."

"And you just couldn't resist looking at it?" I say, seeing that Bill had been in control this whole time.

"I held onto the photos as insurance in case she would need some motivation and *redirection.*" His head tips to one side, and he tacks on, "Of course, I didn't expect you to spend so much time with her. After I found out you were taking her out for a Valentine's weekend, I figured I better stop it somehow. I tried to drop some hints for you to find out her last name or what hockey teams she likes, but you seemed oblivious. I knew you wouldn't believe me, so I wanted to do something to get her to confess to you."

"Aren't you a Sherlock." My tone is steeped in awe as I can't believe I missed his schemes this whole time. There was no dangerous stalker. It was just Bill being Bill.

"I don't know about that." Bill reaches down and scoops up Puck, stroking his back. "I think Puck's pretty good at sneaking around, setting up this whole scheme to get you in here."

Bill and I both pin our gazes on Puck. "You think he did that on purpose? He's just a dog."

"He may be a dog, but he sees exactly what we are all up to, and he knew exactly what to do to bring it to light. He's clearly super intelligent." Bill chuckles, a full smile filling his lips as he adds through his chuckle, "He gets that from me."

Fourteen

Paisley

I made it home super late, but I can't settle down, and I definitely don't sleep. I toss and turn, my stomach a hurricane of knots. My body doesn't even find comfort in the fact that I'm lying in my own place, in my own room, in my own luxurious bed for the first time in a month. After several long hours, I resign myself to the fact that I'm not going to sleep. I kick my blanket down to the bottom of my bed and sit up, flipping on my lamp.

I'm upset I screwed things up with Noah before we even had a chance to try to be anything more than friends. Bigger than that—I'm furious with my dad. He put me up to this whole thing. I had been so blind, only seeing the admiration I would win from him. I was clearly naive.

More than the anger I was feeling, I was also having so much clarity. Something happened in Mapleton that I never expected. I stopped caring about what my dad thought, and I started thinking for myself. Now I want answers. The sun isn't even fully up yet, but that's not going to slow me. I know where to find him. I take a moment to dress and drive over to the gym he both owns and works out at every morning.

I don't even blink an eye when I locate his car pulled up to the curb in the parking lot. It's perfect timing because the club is nearly empty, and we can finally talk. I resist clenching my hands into fists as I make my way inside the building, and my eyes immediately land on my dad on his weight bench, right where I knew he would be.

But he's not alone.

And I'm not surprised.

My breath hitches in the back of my throat when I zoom in on my brother, Peyton, standing by my dad's head, spotting him. They've always been the best of friends, doing everything together, so it shouldn't surprise me they are working out together.

And it doesn't.

It stings to think I can't even find one moment to talk to my dad alone. My steps lose some of the urgency, but I trudge my way over to the bench, forgoing a traditional hello. "Dad."

"Squirt." He leads with the childhood nickname I loathe. "I thought I told you to let me know when you got on the road." His fingers curl around the loaded bar, and he winces as he pushes it up.

"I knew I wouldn't be able to sleep so I ended up driving home last night." I cross my arms over my chest and jut out my foot.

"That's good," he says on his exhale and pauses to inhale as he lowers the bar again. On his extension, he breathes out. "Glad you made it home safe." He quickens his reps, my brother counting them out. They both go about their task like I'm not even standing there.

That's all he has to say to me?

That's good and glad you made it home safe.

I almost destroyed an entire team's reputation because he told me to, and I don't even get a hug.

My cheeks fire hot. So many suppressed emotions bubble to the surface. I'm seeing years of flashbacks, each event the same. My dad and at least one of my brothers, bonding over their shared hobbies, and me standing there—as I am now—an outsider looking in.

Everything I ever wanted to say hangs on the tip of my tongue, and it itches, waiting for a chance to be heard, but I close my mouth and resist.

This isn't about me at all.

My hands fall to my side, and my body is heavier than it was when I came in here. This is about him, and there isn't anything I'll ever do to change that. He could have dictated that hit piece for me. If I had written it verbatim and taken the heat for him, I'd still be standing here feeling disconnected.

The disconnect doesn't hang on much. An overwhelming new emotion washes over me, and all I can think of is—*it's not worth it.*

It's not my job to try to mold him into someone he has never been. The sooner I accept that, the sooner I will be happy. And better than that, I can start living my life for me. I don't even have to swallow all those emotions hanging on the tip of my tongue. As soon as I realize that, the hurt, the anger, the jealousy, the never measuring up—they all float away.

It's crazy how accepting the truth finally sets me free, and I shrug, feeling lighter, and slowly back away from him.

It's crazy early in the morning, and I have nothing to do back at my apartment. Since I'm already here, I scan the empty rows of treadmills and think about how I could use a workout myself as well. It would help to loosen up some of this travel stiffness. I set my eyes on the treadmill in the far corner, and stride over with my shoulders back.

If I'm going to start making choices for me, it's going to start now.

I throw my keys in the treadmill cup holder and turn on the motor to the lowest setting as I stretch my arms high over my head, breathing deep into the muscle stretch. Then I roll my shoulders, feeling the one still stiffer than it should be, and I grab the TV remote and flick on the flatscreen that's in front of me. It's sports news, the only thing dad ever watches. I turn up the volume. It's some sort of Hometown Hero segment. This week's episode is on a minor league baseball team that adopted an underfunded pet shelter. They not only raised enough money to fund it, but they also bought a new building and started a medical fund for low-income pet owners.

It's just dogs, cats, and one pot-bellied pig that is surprisingly domestic, but tears pour out of my eyes. As many times as I wipe them away, I can't keep my eyes dry. I'm overly emotional with everything that happened in Mapleton and with my dad, but this show has that sappy feel-good gut-wrench thing you get when you have renewed hope in people. I'm overcome with so much emotion that I power down my treadmill and jog to the locker room for a tissue to blow my nose.

As I scurry across the gym, sniffing the whole way, I'm reminded of how Bill invited me to their team charity carnival, and how I barely considered it at the time. A wave of goosebumps washes over me, and I know without one doubt that I need to shoot that carnival. Not simply to make it up to them and to myself, but to pay it forward to the community so they can all see there's still good in this world.

My lips pinch tightly together as I hold back a smile. It's too soon to celebrate, but I skip to the locker room, no longer needing a tissue. Instead, I hurry back toward the exit.

"Hey, Paisley," Dad calls out.

I toss a glance over my shoulder right as he sits up on the edge of his bench and takes a towel from Peyton. "Where are you headed?"

"Ah, I have things to do." I drop my gaze to the floor before I add, "And I want to quit the magazine."

I stare at my shoes while I wait for his response, and it doesn't come fast enough. Peyton cuts in, "Is this about Noah?"

I stare off past him, because I don't even know if it is. It's partly about him, but more about me. "Maybe."

Dad shakes his head while dabbing his temples with the corner of the towel, his lips pinched tightly. Against my better judgment, I ask his opinion, "What do you think?"

"I think . . ." He pauses to roll his towel lengthwise and wraps it around the back of his neck as he raises his gaze to mine. "I think that boy's trouble, but I can see by the spark in your eye that you're going to love him anyway."

"Maybe you're right." I offer a weak shrug before I add, "But I think I need to find out for myself."

With that, I spin on my heel and exit the gym with an extra pep in my step. Time to book another Airbnb in Mapleton. I have an event to go to this weekend.

Fifteen

NOAH

Nobody can ever accuse Bill of not loving his team or his community.

It's Saturday, right before noon, but that doesn't mean the sun is shining. It's gray and overcast, with a light wind dancing through the air. I wag my head as I help Bill—per his insistence—drag a twenty-foot inflatable slide to the center of the town square. He rented the entire park, invited every food vendor he knows, hired a band, and even brought in a petting zoo. He also assigned each member of Granite Ice a game booth to work. He ran out of game booths by the time he got to me, so I got roped into the inflatables.

Despite all this fun, the only thing I can think about is Paisley and why I didn't try to stop her from leaving. Anxiety attack or not, I was a jerk for not helping her when she was afraid. Even though it turned out to be Bill, she still doesn't know that. She might still be afraid someone dangerous is coming for her.

In addition to that, I haven't had time to deal with Bill or even process how messed up what he did was, but that hasn't stopped him from acting like he owns me. When we have the slide spread out, I grab the security strap closest to me and call to him, "Did you bring the stakes?"

"Ah, I'm letting Red Barn Kabobs handle those." His lips bend up at his joke, but his gaze is down, as he's focused on plugging the air compressor hose into the slide.

"Ha ha." I fake laugh, giving him time to get over his own joke.

He pats his coat pocket. "I must have left them in the trailer." He jerks his thumb over his shoulder back to the parking lot. "Want to run and grab them?"

"I can . . ." I pause and watch Bill crank on the air compressor, the sound filling the space between us, drowning out the warning I was going to give him about waiting to fill the slide until it's properly grounded.

I sigh, letting it go.

This is Bill I'm talking to.

He does things his own way—the hard way.

The best use of my time is to get the stakes as quickly as possible. I spin on my heel and jog back through the game booths that are already filled with kids.

As I head back, a steady stream of families, couples, and even teens filter into the park. Everyone is laughing and enjoying the day. I admit I was dreading today—as it's an awful lot of work to throw a carnival—but now that everything is coming together, I can't help but feel proud to be a small part of it.

I scan the parking lot for Bill's truck and trailer and I find it backed up against the sidewalk. I pick up my pace and scurry over. Unlocking the back, I find the stakes all tie wrapped together on the floor. That's easy enough. I grab them and turn to hustle back.

As I cut back through the thickening crowd, a sense of nostalgia washes over me. Memories of my childhood spent playing in this park, specifically hockey on the pond when it was frozen, flood back. I pause in front of the little pond. Kids skate in circles, passing a hockey puck back and forth to Jackson, who got put on pond hockey duty. It's cute to see the kids swing their sticks back and slam the pucks as hard as they can to Jackson, who pretends to miss each goal. He lets out fake animated sighs of disappointment. The kids all pile around him, each one beaming with a full smile.

Across the pond, Axl and Sophie are crossing the park with arms linked together, coming this way. They make me think of Paisley. It would be fun to experience this with her. I take a deep breath, savoring how I can easily do that again now that my meds are finally working.

It's funny how I had started to think this team was lame, but when I'm forced to take a step back and look at the big picture, this team and what it does for the community is pretty amazing. I bite my bottom lip, now seeing that my feelings of apprehension had nothing to do with the team, or even Bill. It had everything to do with my desire not to feel as if my life was out of my control.

"Hey." Axl jogs up next to me, nodding toward the pond. "Think you can take on those kids?"

"I don't know," I say with a chuckle. "They aren't going easy on Jackson."

Axl snickers while his face takes a more neutral expression. "I wanted to talk to you about something."

"Oh, yeah?" I pull my gaze away from the kids to Axl. The sounds of sticks slamming against the pucks echo in the distance. "What about?"

"It's about my apartment." He nods across the street at the old building. "As you know, Sophie and I are getting married. We found a house we want to buy outside of town on five acres. I stupidly renewed my lease a couple of months ago. I was wondering if there's any way you'd want to sublet it." His expression takes on a mischievous smile. "Unless you like living with Bill?"

"Funny." I cut my gaze back to his apartment building, having never considered it before. Most of the guys live close to the arena in new apartments, but those are so expensive. This building is old and perhaps affordable . . . "What do you pay?"

"Only six hundred, but it comes with a pet mouse, and you have to promise not to kill him because he's actually cool. You also must feed him at least once a day, but he surprisingly doesn't like cheese. He prefers peanuts or dark chocolate—" He interrupts himself and tacks on, "The dark chocolate is Sophie's fault."

I stuff my hands in my coat pockets as the wind picks up, and my brow furrows in concentration. I have been meaning to do something about my living situation. I'm not going to find anything for less than six hundred. It really is a no brainer, and I nod. "Yeah, that sounds great. When are you moving—"

A shrill scream spirals from somewhere in the crowd right as a massive gust of wind rips through the park. I take a step back to keep my balance. A ripple of litter cascades through the park as the wind steals napkins from vendors and even a loosely held stroller from a mother. The mom quickly catches it, but my gaze is pulled to another even bigger issue . . .

The slide!

It's partially inflated and has lifted off the ground like a massive balloon, only held down by the hose that's attached to the air compressor.

I forgot about Bill!

Axl sees it too, and we take off together.

Bill has been swallowed up by the slide, flattened on the ground, with only his boots sticking out the side. "Bill, just hold still," I call out, dropping down to the ground by his feet and lifting the slide. Axl comes in beside me, and together we shimmy it off of him before Bill incurs more than a bruised ego.

When he sits up, he wobbles, and the crowd of people surrounding us cheers. We got lucky, and we don't need to fight about whose fault it is. I hold my hand out to help him up. "Glad you're okay."

The wind howls, rolling through the park, and Axl extends his hand to me. "Give me one of those stakes. We need to get this pinned down fast."

I hand them out, and we scurry around the slide, but it's as if the weather is mocking our efforts. As soon as the last stake is in, the sky opens, dumping out the hugest snowflakes. It's a full-blown blizzard, and people run toward the parking lot back to their cars. Axl takes off back through the crowd to find Sophie, and Bill mumbles his way back to his truck.

I should be moving too, but I can't.

Someone is blocking me.

Someone wearing all black—from her midnight trench coat to her combat books.

Even though she has a hand over her face, shielding it from the snow, it doesn't conceal who it is. Paisley.

My heart ticks up a notch seeing her. I so want her to be here for the right reasons, but I'm guarded. "What are you doing here?" I ask. "Don't tell me you got a photo of Bill under that slide?"

Her lips fold in, and she shakes her head. "I wouldn't embarrass him like that."

I don't have anything to add, but I study the inflection in her eyes. They look honest when she adds, "I got a bunch of great photos of you guys. I'm going to write an article on all the charity work you guys do."

"Hmm." I shove my hands in my pockets, still trying to understand everything that has happened. My heart is so attuned to her nearness, it hammers against my chest, but I am still so conflicted.

"I quit my dad's magazine."

My brows dip down.

"I know I can't use the magazine as an excuse. I had my own choices to make, but I never want to do anything like that again. I'm going to start my own photography series that highlights sports teams and their community involvement." She shakes her head, and no words come out for a long beat. Then tear-stained words tumble out of her mouth. "Haven't you ever made a mistake?"

I do everything I can to ignore that I almost got Bill killed by getting distracted on my way back from getting the stakes—that being only one of the many, many things I've done wrong. Like leaving my meds out for Puck to grab more than once. He could have died if he'd swallowed them.

I've made so many mistakes.

I scratch the back of my head, pushing all the thoughts away.

She has a point.

Plus, she's standing in a blizzard, and I can't help but think she's the most beautiful woman I've ever seen. I don't want to be bitter. That's not my nature. One of the reasons I reacted as harshly as I did was because I was having an anxiety attack.

Things are clearer now.

So much clearer.

When I look at her . . . she feels like mine.

I nod, slowly, as I watch the flakes accumulating on her hair, making her even more stunning. "I've made mistakes." I step closer, closing the space between us, and stare into her fiery eyes. "I shouldn't have reacted the way I did. The truth is that I suffer from anxiety, and I was having an attack. If I had been thinking clear, I would have never let you leave. I'm sorry too." Her eyes grow even warmer, not for a second losing that fiery spark. I could go on and on to further explain about my anxiety attack, but words don't sound that appealing to me.

I have a better idea.

One to get us back together faster.

I drop my hand to her waist, pulling her to me, and lower my face until our lips crash together. Hungrily, she kisses me back. Adrenaline floods my veins, fueling a direct shot to my heart.

Epilogue

About a month later . . .

The servers pass out the last of the cheesecake, and saliva pools in the center of my mouth when I finally get my slice. Strawberry mounds with berry sauce drip all over the cake. It's the most delicious thing I've seen in a long time, and right as I ready my fork to stab it, Noah cuts my concentration. "Easy there."

I flick my gaze to him and speak through gritted teeth. "Nothing like being the last ones served dessert at a dinner party of five hundred. I thought I was going to pass out watching all these calorie-counting Karens take one measly bite of their slice and push it aside all while I had no cake."

"I noticed that too." Noah nods to the table directly across from us, where every piece was left untouched. "Look at that offense."

"Twelve pieces discarded like trash," I seethe. I can't even look at it, as it almost brings a tear to my eye. I cut my focus back to my delible slice, and Noah elbows me.

"Sophie's coming." He stands, pulling my chair out for me, and I shoot one more look of longing at my cake before I rise. Sophie glides forward as she reaches her arms out. "Thank you so much for coming, guys."

"Congratulations." I lean in for a hug. Sophie is one of the most beautiful brides I've ever seen with her princess ballgown and traditional veil. You'd think for a celebrity, she'd have selected some New York hotel or tropical destination wedding. When it came down to her special day—friends and family were the biggest pull, and she brought the reception right here to Mapleton. It's the first chance I've gotten to talk to her, as she's been constantly swarmed with everyone. "I've never seen a more stunning venue."

"I always pictured myself having a movie-perfect New England wedding," she confesses, her eyes sparkling as she admires the old manor courtyard decorated in ivy and magnolias. "I wanted the burgundy wines, the satin gowns, the whole black-tie to-do. Something that's timeless and would inspire me every time I look at my photos."

"I definitely think you nailed the venue." My gaze follows the trail her own gaze sets, as the hundreds of tea lights seem to shine so much brighter when they are set against a French Country tablecloth under the tents.

"I'm so glad you both made it." Her gaze lifts to Noah, bringing him into the conversation.

"We wouldn't dream of missing it." Noah leans in for a quick hug, adding, "Congratulations." He looks good in a tux, and seeing him in this wedding backdrop does not help my overreactive imagination from thinking that maybe, someday, we'd be here, too.

The live band switches their song, bringing the tempo down, and the couples respond by flocking to the dance floor. Sophie's gaze sweeps back over the dance floor, and a regretful smile tugs on her lips. "Sorry, but I'm going to have to excuse myself to find my groom. This is one of my favorite songs to dance to."

"No apologies." I wave her off, and I smile as she weaves her way back through the crowd, her dress glittering under the muted lighting.

Noah extends his hand in offering. "Shall we?"

"Oh, I don't dance." My head springs back, my eyes rounding in alarm.

A chuckle leaks from his mouth. "Is this about the mosh pit?"

"No." I shake my head adamantly. "It has nothing to do with that, although that certainly didn't help."

"Come on." His genuine smile finds me, the one that makes the lines by his eyes crease, and he extends his hand out further. "One dance."

I give him a side-eye, and if he didn't look so handsome, I would have an easier time saying no, but I don't dance. Plus, crowds are not my thing. Not to mention my cheesecake is on the table, calling my name. I can't help but stare at it.

There's so much empathy spiraling out of his eyes. "You don't want to leave your cake, do you?"

"No." I gesture toward it. "What if the busboy thinks I've discarded it and takes it?"

"I feel that so much in my soul." There's an air of teasing in his tone when he nods toward the table. "Let's do this properly then. First, you eat the cake, and then we dance to the next song."

It's silly, but a wave of relief washes over me. I plop back down on my chair, taking my napkin into my lap, but he just sits there, his cake untouched. "Are you going to eat that?"

His gaze drops to his cake, then bounces to me. "I was going to save it for you."

Never in my life did my heart slam against my ribcage so fast. There have been so many signs along the way that Noah is the one for me. None have been greater than this. "I don't know what to say." I blink, and the emotions clog my throat. "This is the second time you've given me your cheesecake. I should feel bad, but I can't because I'm just so happy."

He grabs my fork and hands it to me. "Well, you know how it goes." He winks, a gleam sparking out of the corner of his eye. "You're going to have to make it up to me."

"Now what do you want?" I tease, knowing these wagers have usually worked in my favor.

He's quiet for a long moment, his gaze dropping to his lap before raising it again, and he smiles my favorite smile. "I'll let you know very soon . . ."

BONUS EPILOGUE

Jackson Owen

"Bill Baker!" Noah yells before he bursts through the locker room doors. His mouth opens in a pant, and he scans the room. "Have you seen Bill?"

"Ah, no." I shake my head as I dig through my locker again, looking for my lucky glove. I never used to lose any of my stuff, but ever since my last breakup, my mind has been so distracted. I lost my glove last week before the game, and Bill grabbed a new one for me. It turned out that was a super lucky glove because we won that game. I definitely don't want to lose it. A knot swells in my throat when I lift my hockey bag again and look under it. Something drops to the floor. I don't even need to check to know it's my lucky glove. A sigh of relief falls from my lips.

I stuff my glove into my hockey bag and shift my gaze to Noah, who sniffs around the locker room like a bloodhound. "What's up, bruh?" I take a step back, hugging the lockers, as sometimes he gets like this when he's off his meds. "You okay?"

"No." His eyes are glossed over, and his face is crimson as he spins on his heel and shouts toward Bill's office. "Bill, you'd better get out here!"

I swallow, not understanding how he could talk to his boss like that, and doubting that Bill is even here. Everybody left but me, and I'm only here because I've been scouring the place for my glove.

A shuffle from the door pulls both Noah's and my attention that way. It's Bill, dressed in head-to-toe Granite Ice warmup clothes. He leans against the wall and crosses his arms in front of him as if he's preparing for a confrontation.

"Tell me you didn't," Noah hisses, his expression so full of hatred that I do a double take. This is not the Noah I know. I'm about to push my hand on his chest to hold him back. He looks as if he's about to attack Bill.

"Noah," Bill says calmly. "I love you like a son, but I can't have you on my team while you're dating Blake's daughter."

My gaze bounces from Bill to Noah as I struggle to fill in the gaps. Noah blurts out everything I need to know. "You traded me." Noah's arms flail around as if he's having trouble controlling his body. "To some brand-new team nobody has even heard of."

"It's going to work out just fine." Bill's words are cool and measured. "You wanted to move out of the house and have your own life, didn't you? Well, this will get you all the way to Long Island. I traded you to Blake Anton's new team."

My jaw plummets all the way down.

Bill has lost his mind.

"Blake doesn't have a team." Noah rushes out, wild arm gestures continue to fly all around him. "And even if he did, why would you trade me?"

"Now you get to be with Paisley." Bill's smooth gesture seems almost condescending when paired with how upset Noah is. "Isn't that what you wanted?"

"N-no. It's not what I wanted. What I wanted was for you to accept Paisley as part of my life—the same way I accepted you as part of my mom's life." Noah stutters for a moment before spouting off, "This trade makes us rivals."

"No." Bill tips his head coyly at Noah. "You made us rivals when you started dating that woman."

Lightning could crash into this locker room, and it would be less shocking than what I'm seeing. I knew Noah had a new girlfriend, but I had no idea about the conflict going on behind the scenes. The tension in the air is palpable, and my gaze bounces from Noah to Bill.

"Whatever," Noah mutters as he slams his fist into a nearby locker. The echo fills the room. He doesn't wait for it to quiet before he storms out of the room, calling back, "You thought you were losers before, just wait until we meet again on the ice . . ."

Well, this is awkward. I tap my finger on my leg, pretending I didn't just witness the single most terrifying thing to go down since I joined this team. Bill is staring after the trail Noah left, and his cheeks are redder than a firetruck.

One thing I've learned about Bill is that you never want to cross him. I hug my hockey bag close to my chest, peeking inside to check for my glove. No relief comes over me this time, as the stakes have just been raised.

I might need two lucky gloves for next season . . .

Follow Jackson in his unending quest for love and his lucky glove, in *All I Need is My Glove.*

About J.P. Sterling

J.P. Sterling grew up watching old reruns of Lucille Ball and Mary Tyler Moore and fell in love with wholesome entertainment and slapstick comedy. She loves leaning into the over-the-top humor and full circle moments, especially if it means the underdog gets to shine.

Aside from writing, she's also a wife and homeschooling mom, a holistic dietitian, a former college professor and lover of all-things dark chocolate.

*No swears. Just kisses. No Blasphemies. *

Let's get social!

Hey you amazing reader! You are invited to join my private reader group for all-things clean books and friends. Enter the group here: https://www.facebook.com/groups/1500850764081965

Other places to follow me:

Instagram: https://www.instagram.com/stories/authorjpsterling/

Facebook: https://www.facebook.com/jpsterlingauthor/

Amazon: https://www.amazon.com/stores/author/B01N9TJXJN/about

Also by J.P. Sterling

<u>Christmas Shenanigans (All Standalones)</u>

Mingle All the Way

Tis the Season to Get Married

Let's Not and Sleigh We Did

<u>The Coffee Loft Series (All Standalones)</u>

Pardon My French Press

No More Mr. Chia Guy

Truely, Madly, Steeply Brew (coming 1/25)

<u>Sweet Hockey RomCom (All Standalones)</u>

The Pucker-Up Pact

Shot Through the Heart

All I Need is my Glove (Coming 2025)

<u>A Modern Fairy Tale Series (All Standalones)</u>

Royally Rugged

<u>Bosses and Billionaires Series (All Standalones)</u>

Maid for my Billionaire Boss

Upcycling My Rig-Pig Boss

Kissed by My Billionaire Boss

Marooned with My Celebrity Boss

<u>A Heart that Dances Series</u>

Dancing on Broken Ankles

The Stars We See

A Heart that Dances

A Heart that Loves

<u>Water and Stone Duet</u>

Ruby in the Water

Lily in the Stone

Acknowledgements

Special thanks to my friend and fellow hockey romance author, Kerry Evelyn for walking with me on this hockey romance journey.

I also have to thank my editing team, especially Darcy for his expertise with the hockey sequences.

My little family.

All my readers and the entire books community. It's an honor to have a little corner in this space. It really does feel more like an extended family than any "job" I've ever had.

To my writing partner, Brooks. I would have never made it past book one without you.

And to my Father in Heaven, who writes my story better than I ever could.